"The author lived a summer similar to the one described in this book. Her re-creation of that world is done with loving attention to the beauty and gentleness that were a part of that time."—St. Louis *Post-Dispatch*

"A high-water mark, both as a family story and as a period piece."—*Saturday Review*

"A serene, old-fashioned charm lights THE HALF SISTERS. Every middle child will sympathize with Luvvy's anguished hope."—Chicago *Tribune*

"Girls will love this novel . . . about a 12-year-old girl who longs to be accepted by her older sisters."—*Commonweal*

"Mrs. Carlson has created a vibrant, heartwarming portrait of another era—and a summer of growing up that was filled with laughter and sadness."—Galesburg *Register-Mail*

". . . the story of a very lively, normal little girl in the early part of the present century. The author brings her usual skill to her creation of a very real family, all of whose members have individuality and charm."—*School Library Journal*

The Half Sisters

by NATALIE SAVAGE CARLSON

Pictures by THOMAS di GRAZIA

A HARPER TROPHY BOOK

Harper & Row, Publishers
New York, Evanston, San Francisco, London

THE HALF SISTERS

Text copyright © 1970 by Natalie Savage Carlson

Pictures copyright © 1970 by Thomas di Grazia

First published in 1970. 3rd printing, 1971.

Standard Book Number: 06–440017–4

For the Girls
Amelia, Mary Hester, and Josie

and the Children
Eve and Vangie

with memories of *Francie and Joe*

Some Other Books
by Natalie Savage Carlson

Contents

The Half Sisters

I

Waiting for the Girls

"*Today is going to be* the happiest day of my life," Luvvy Savage told her little sister Maudie.

It was a morning in early June of 1915.

"Is Mama coming home?" asked Maudie anxiously.

"Mama and Papa and the Girls," pronounced Luvvy. "Why do you think you're wearing your best dress? Mama and Papa have only been gone to Frederick for two days, but the Girls have been away since Christmas vacation. You remember they couldn't come home Easter because they were in the infirmary, with the measles."

"Why don't they go to Miss Harriet's school with us?" asked Maudie. "Then they wouldn't have to go away."

"They're too old to be tutored by Miss Harriet," explained Luvvy, "and they've been going to the convent ever since their mother died anyhow."

Maudie's face, beneath the huge blue bow, looked more woeful. "Did Mama die?" Her little mouth began to turn down.

"No, silly. Didn't I tell you she's coming home today? The Girls are our half sisters, so they belong to Papa. But they don't belong to Mama. Only you and I and Marylou belong to Mama."

"Then why did Mama leave us and go to their school?"

"Because she's their mother now—their Mama Della —so she wanted to see Regina graduate and Hetty get her gold medal for deportment and hear Betsey recite 'Lord Ullin's Daughter.' Because Mama is proud of them too."

Luvvy—seldom called Luvena—sighed with exasperation. Maudie never seemed to realize that Papa had married the Girls' mother first. All the little seven-year-old understood was that Regina and Hetty and Betsey were the Girls. And she and Luvvy and three-year-old Marylou were the Children. That is, Luvvy *had* been one of the Children, but everything would be different this summer. She was going to be twelve in July, and that should make her one of the Girls.

The Savages lived on a farm in western Maryland.

The fields and orchards puckered into hills, with the mountains on one side and the Potomac River on the other. Across the river were the Blue Ridge Mountains of Virginia, and when Luvvy rode the horse up the road, she soon reached the Harpers Ferry bridge, where both states and West Virginia were wedged together—like three slices of a pie.

The stone part of their home, Shady Grove, had been built in 1804 as a coaching stop. Its porches had lacy white banisters. Its windows, set into walls three feet thick, were so deeply recessed that Luvvy often sat sideways on one of their sills to read or study. A later owner had added white frame wings on each side in 1900, so the house was large enough to accommodate some of the people who worked on the farm since Papa took the train to his tool factory in Hagerstown every weekday.

"Why don't they get home?" Maudie asked Luvvy for the third time.

"I've told you a hundred times already that I don't know. Maybe they started home late."

Luvvy felt as impatient as her little sister, but she was trying not to show it. Perhaps she could do something to make the time pass faster. Then she thought of the dolls. She had put them away in the little attic trunk because if the Girls were to accept her as one of them, she must never play with dolls anymore. But the time

5

was dragging so, perhaps she could take them out of the trunk for just one last time.

First she must get rid of Maudie so she wouldn't be tattling to the Girls about the dolls.

"I'm going to take a nap until they come," she said. "You can go out and play with Marylou."

Maudie made no move to leave.

Luvvy stiffly stretched herself out on the old horse-hair sofa. She clasped her hands across her breast and closed her eyes.

"Are you asleep yet, Luvvy?" asked Maudie.

There was no reply—only heavy breathing from Luvvy. Maudie leaned over her and stared at her closed eyes.

"I don't think you're really asleep. I can see your eyelids move."

Luvvy squeezed her eyelids tightly and began to snore loudly. Maudie watched for a while with a doubtful look on her face. At last she turned away. Luvvy heard her footsteps going down the hall. The big oak door squeaked, then slammed.

Luvvy jumped up and hurried to the hall. She tiptoed up the two flights of steps to the attic landing. She turned past the door of the cook's bedroom and opened the one to the south room, with its big dormer windows.

This was Luvvy's playroom. It was a cheerful room with whitewashed walls and floor closets set under the eaves. Except for a few discarded pieces of furniture,

6

it was bare, so there was plenty of room for any kind of a game.

Luvvy pulled the trunk from under the bed frame and took out three small bisque dolls. They were Lady Jane Grey, Fair Rosamund, and Maid Marian, and they had been purchased at the notion store in Brunswick, the nearest town of any size.

"Now we're going to have a big dance, just like we'll have when the Girls are home," Luvvy promised the dolls. "There will be a lot of parties from now on, but this will be your last one."

She dressed the dolls in their fanciest clothes, made from scraps of silk, satin, and lace. Regina had sewed the bonnet that Luvvy put on Lady Jane Grey's hard bisque curls, trimming it with a bluebird feather that Luvvy had found in the garden.

The dolls were set carefully in a row against the wall. Luvvy seated herself in the old rocking chair that had belonged to Grandma Savage. She rocked slowly back and forth, her eyes fixed on the dolls. She began to imagine the dance.

Three gray mice, dressed in green velvet suits, came marching out of the floor closet. Each bowed before a doll.

"May I have the honor of this dance, Miss Jane?"

"I believe I have the good fortune to be your partner for the next waltz, Miss Rosamund."

"At your service, Miss Marian."

7

Luvvy was remembering the things that the young men said to the young ladies when she'd eavesdropped at the dances held at Shady Grove.

She began to hum "The Blue Danube." The mice gentlemen swung their partners out onto the attic floor. They bowed and dipped and glided to Luvvy's music.

A discordant note rose above the tune.

"Luvvy, Luvvy," whined a childish voice. It was way down on the second-floor landing, but it plaintively carried to the attic room. Luvvy hummed more softly. "Luvvy, Luvvy!" It was at the top of the stairs. Then the door opened. "There you are!"

Maudie stood in the doorway, triumphantly, her old rag doll hanging from one hand. Luvvy scowled at her. The mice gentlemen scurried back into the dark closet. The little dolls sat stiffly against the wall again.

"What do you want?" asked Luvvy in an irritated voice.

"Can I play with you?" begged Maudie. "Can Little Mary Sparagrass play with your dolls?"

"No!" snapped Luvvy. "You don't play the same way we do. We're having a dance, and we don't want to be bothered."

Maudie looked at the dolls. "They aren't dancing or doing anything."

"That shows you don't have enough imagination to play with me. Why don't you go down to the porch

and have a tea party with Little Mary Sparagrass?"

"I want to be with you."

Luvvy was too annoyed to feel flattered. "I don't want to be with you," she stated rudely.

Tears glistened in Maudie's eyes. One ran down her cheek.

"Oh, don't bawl," said Luvvy, ashamed. In a kinder voice, she said, "But I'm not going to play with the dolls anymore. I'm going to put them back in the trunk forever." She began to do so. "I tell you what, Maudie. How would you like to climb out on the roof with me and look down the valley to see if the Machine is coming?"

Maudie nodded eagerly and dropped Little Mary Sparagrass on the floor.

"You'll play with me sometimes even when the Girls are home, won't you?" asked Maudie. "You're always running after Betsey when she's here."

"Maudie, there will be only *two* years difference between me and Betsey after my birthday, but you will be *five* years younger. Besides, I act older now so Betsey will want me with her."

"We don't have to play dolls," persisted Maudie. "We can play whatever you want."

"I've been playing with you and going to school with you all year while the Girls were gone. Didn't I let you ride behind me on Dolly lots of times? And didn't I show you the muskrat holes in the pond? And didn't I take you and Marylou down to the barn to see the new colt on Pansy's day off?"

"Mama made you take us to see the colt."

"She isn't making me take you out on the roof, is she? And if you tell her about it, I'll never take you out there again. It's dangerous for a little child like you."

Being on the roof was like looking down at the earth from heaven. The many old trees laid a mantle of shadows on the front lawn. They could see all the way over them to where the valley opened out at Weverton. They could see snips of the Potomac River and the Chesapeake & Ohio Canal and the dirt road. But there was no automobile on the road. If there had been, it would surely be Papa driving the Machine home because they were the only people for miles around who owned an automobile.

The June air was soft and warm. Its breeze felt like lukewarm water flowing across Luvvy's face. There was a warm smell in the air too, of fresh earth and growing things mixed with a weedy whiff that came from the river and the canal. Everything was green—the light green of the cornfield and orchard trees, the dark green of the river, and the blue-green of the mountains on the Virginia side.

"Why don't we see them coming?" asked Maudie.

"Because they aren't there yet, that's why. Now

don't sit down on the shingles and get your white dress all dirty or Mama will blame me. Squat on your feet."

Luvvy walked slowly up to the rooftree, and Maudie started to follow her.

"Stay where you are," ordered Luvvy. "You might slip and fall off. I just want to look at the peach orchard."

She shaded her eyes. All the pink blossoms were gone, and in their place were green leaves. Faint sounds came from the orchard trees—the chittering of black-birds and the moaning of mourning doves. Luvvy listened closely. Were those her special doves calling back and forth to each other? When would their nestlings be big enough for her to bring home and raise as pets? Caring for a pair of doves would keep her from being tempted to play with dolls.

It seemed that she was always waiting for something that took ages to happen, like waiting to be twelve years old. Waiting was the worst torment in the world, especially having to wait to see if the Girls would accept her as one of them this time.

"Now let's climb inside and go down to Pansy and Marylou," suggested Luvvy. "The family will surely be here soon, and we don't want to be up on the roof when they arrive."

She helped Maudie climb through the dormer window. The two went down the stairs and out the front door.

Pansy was weaving a necklace of the dandelions the little girl was picking on the lawn. Three-year-old Marylou had a mop of tight curls that was the envy of all her sisters.

The hired girl had a worried look on her freckled face. "Something awful must have happened to your folks. Maybe they got hit by a train at one of the crossings. Two people got killed at the Knoxville crossing last week."

The very thought chilled Luvvy. "But it's about twenty miles to Frederick," she pointed out. "It always takes an hour anyhow, and maybe they slept late. It would probably take a whole day to drive there in the buggy."

"Perhaps they decided to stay another day," said Pansy.

This seemed almost as disastrous to Luvvy as an accident.

"I think I'll go to the orchard and see my doves," she said. "Then when I get back, they should be driving up."

"I'll go with you," said Maudie.

"No," Luvvy said. "You'll make a lot of noise and scare the big birds."

"You stay with Marylou and me," suggested Pansy to Maudie. "If they don't get here in another fifteen minutes, I'll have to give you your dinner."

13

"With some cake?" asked Maudie.

"A big slice of that beautiful Lady Baltimore cake you like so much. All full of fruit and nuts. Your mother made it herself before she left."

Maudie hopefully followed Pansy and Marylou inside. This was Luvvy's chance to sneak quietly off by herself. She went past the grape-arbor wall, up the steep hill of the apple orchard to the rail fence that separated it from the peach orchard. She crawled through the rails, counted three rows of trees to the right, then walked between the trees.

She had really intended only to stand under the tree and look up at the nest since she was wearing her good white dress. Sometimes the little doves stuck their slender beaks over the edge. Often she could see the long tail of one of the parents. But there was no sign of life above.

Luvvy began to worry. Perhaps they had already grown up and flown away. She was filled with anxiety. She must climb up and see if they were still there. She would try to keep her dress away from the bark.

It wasn't too far to the first crotch. She took off her slippers and carefully set them near the trunk. Then she pulled herself up by her arms, digging her stockinged toes into the rough bark. Slowly she began to crawl out on the branch toward the nest. She pulled her skirt above her knees, but it kept falling down.

14

She breathed a sigh of relief. The two little doves were in the loose nest. They were still covered with pinfeathers, but Luvvy was pleased to see that they were already sprouting soft brown barbs. It seemed ages since they had been just two white eggs.

Suddenly she heard the singing of wings nearby. The mother dove was flying from one tree to another in alarm.

Luvvy began backing along the branch. The mother would want to feed the little ones. She fed them differently than the other birds. Instead of dropping bugs into their open beaks as the blackbirds did, she thrust her bill into theirs and pumped juice from her craw. "Pigeon milk," Sam Crigley, the hired man, called it. That was why Luvvy didn't dare take the little doves home until they were big enough to eat grain from her fingers.

A call that was neither the chirr of a blackbird nor the moan of a dove floated up the hill of the apple orchard.

"Luvvy, Luvvy," it cried as mournfully as a dove.

Luvvy was so angry that she forgot her dress and red sash. As she slid down the tree her sash caught on a sharp twig and snagged. Her dress scraped along the trunk. She hurried toward the fence. She didn't want Maudie to know where the doves' nest was.

"Luvvy, Luvvy! Where are you?" Maudie reached the rail fence first. "Oh, there you are!"

Luvvy looked down at her soiled, wrinkled dress and torn sash with dismay. "See what you've made me do—yelling like that!"

"They've come, Luvvy!" cried Maudie excitedly. "They're home!"

II

The Girls

Luvvy raced down the orchard hill with her torn sash flying like the tail of a kite.

"Wait for me," cried Maudie, whose legs weren't long enough to keep up. "Wait for me."

Papa was taking suitcases from the Machine. "You can drive the wagon down to the depot for the trunks this afternoon," he called over his shoulder to Sam. Then he dropped both suitcases to catch Luvvy as she made a flying leap at him.

"Papa, Papa! I'm so glad you all got back safe. Where's Mama?"

"She's probably in the dining room, seeing about

17

dinner. All your mother thinks about is seeing that this family doesn't starve."

It always seemed impossible that Papa was twenty years older than Mama. But perhaps that was why his hair was graying at the temples and he was spending fewer hours at the factory each day.

Luvvy gave him a double kiss, then broke away and made a beeline for the front porch. The screen door at the far right opened onto the dining room, and there was Mama, helping Pansy add last touches to the table settings.

Mama was a short plump woman with blue-black hair. Papa always said that she had the cheeks of a Winesap apple and the disposition of a spring robin.

Luvvy threw her arm around her. "Mama! You've been gone so long."

"Only two days," Mama pointed out, hugging her tightly.

"But when you're gone two days it seems like weeks," protested Luvvy. "And Martha's so cranky. And Pansy isn't any fun."

"Then maybe it's a good thing for you to miss me for a while so you can appreciate me more when I return." Mama's dimples were playing hide-and-seek as she talked. The children always took their problems to Papa, but it was Mama they sought when they had sorrows.

"Where are the Girls?" asked Luvvy. "I've missed

them too, but I'm used to having them away most of the time."

"In their room, freshening up for dinner after the ride. It was so dusty, and we had a blowout on the Petersville Pike. It took your father almost half an hour to patch the tire. I prefer horses. They're more dependable."

Maudie, who had joined them, stayed with Mama, because she had already greeted the others. Luvvy tore through the downstairs sitting room, across the main hall, through the lower guest room to the other hall, then past the parlor door and up the stairs. It was always a long way from one part of the house to the other.

She even forgot to knock at the door of the Girls' room as they had always demanded. She burst in, to see Regina brushing her long silky hair in front of the bureau. Regina was the Beauty of the family.

She tossed back her hair to give Luvvy a big kiss; then she gave her an affectionate spank with the back of the brush. "How you've grown since I last saw you!"

Luvvy was delighted. "I'm practically twelve," she announced. "And, Regina, you're even prettier than ever." Luvvy looked in the mirror at her own reflection. She was sunburned, and her black hair hung in heavy braids. "No wonder everybody says I look like a gypsy," she said.

Hetty threw her arms around Luvvy.

"Don't worry about your looks, honey," she said. "Pretty is as pretty does. And since I'm plain, I try to be as neat as possible."

Luvvy found herself saying something she had been thinking for a long time. "But you *aren't* plain. I wish I had big blue eyes like yours. And you'd be real pretty if you didn't skin your hair back so tight. When it comes loose, it curls. But I never could have curls. Even when I put my hair up in rags, it just turns out like twisted ropes."

Hetty playfully tugged at one of Luvvy's braids. "But I like my hair to stay in place and not fly around."

That was why Hetty was known as the Neat One.

Betsey turned from the big bowl on the commode, where she was washing her hands. She dried them quickly, then hurried to give Luvvy a hug and kiss.

"We've missed you all terribly," she said. "My, it's good to see you again. Have you missed me?"

Luvvy nodded. She felt that she had missed Betsey most. Regina and Hetty seemed so old and superior, but Betsey was only fourteen.

Betsey was bubbling with the joy of being home. "My, it's wonderful to be back for the whole summer. I get so sick of being bossed by the nuns and cooped up in that place. I wish I had graduated this year."

Chubby Betsey, with her big brown eyes, was the Rebellious One.

I'm more like her than the other two, thought Luvvy.

20

She makes mistakes and says what she thinks, and we both like the same things—horses and buckwheat cakes and playing games. If only Betsey would let me feel close to her, I'd really be one of the Girls.

Regina thoughtfully stared into the mirror. "May O'Brien and I couldn't help crying when we went up for our diplomas. We hated to be leaving the nuns forever."

Regina was beautiful and remote, like the nuns at Frederick. There was something about them that put them above other women, although it wasn't actually beauty. And Hetty always seemed to be standing in Regina's shadow. If she'd only step into the light and be herself.

"I'm glad to be away from them," declared Betsey. "We couldn't even walk into town without one of them tagging along with us," she told Luvvy. "And I don't see why they won't let us eat candy on the street."

That reminded Hetty of something. She picked up a paper sack from her brass bed and handed it to Luvvy. "I brought you a present. Operas. You're always asking about them."

The "operas" were candies that the Girls bought at Miss Beckley's candy shop in Frederick. The name had intrigued Luvvy, so it was disappointing to see that they were only taffy twisted in wax paper. She had imagined that any candy with such an elegant name would be full of nuts and chocolate and maybe coconut.

But the first one she chewed had a delicious flavor.

"You are to share them with the other children," Hetty explained.

What did she mean by the "other" children? Hadn't she noticed that Luvvy was quite grown-up now?

"I'll save most of them for the children," said Luvvy. "Maudie and Marylou love candy. I really used to eat too much of it when I was a child." She wondered why the Girls laughed. Then she suddenly remembered something important. "The medal, Hetty! Can I see your medal?"

"*May* I," Hetty corrected her. "It is quite possible for you to see my medal because it's right here on my shirtwaist."

She obligingly unpinned the medal and handed it to Luvvy. "Don't get finger marks on it," she warned. "Your hands don't look too clean."

Luvvy held the gold medal in a flattened palm. "Oo-oh!" She drew in her breath reverently. "It's so bright and shiny, and it says 'Excellence in Deportment.' I wish I could go to the convent and win a medal like this. I'd study hard and always be obedient and keep my clothes neat."

"They certainly don't look neat now," Hetty said gently. "And you've torn your sash. Come here and let me see if it can be mended."

"I had to climb a tree to see if my doves were still

there. But I wouldn't be climbing trees at the convent."

Hetty looked at Betsey. "And your hair needs combing again after that windy ride."

"Oh, pshaw!" exclaimed Betsey. "I'm home now, so I can look how I want."

"You mustn't say 'pshaw,' Betsey," reproved Hetty. "Slang is unladylike."

Luvvy decided it was important to take sides with Betsey.

"What's wrong with 'pshaw'?" she asked. "There's a Mrs. Shaw in Sandy Hook who's doing our washing now. Oh, Shaw, Mrs. Shaw, how is Mr. Shaw and all the little Shaws?"

All three of the Girls laughed. Luvvy felt quite clever. They seemed to be enjoying her grown-up company.

"I'm going to have Sister Mary Pauline for my teacher next year," said Hetty. "She's my favorite. I adore her."

Luvvy adored all the nuns in their black habits and snowy barbettes. She thought of their brown rosaries, with the heavy wooden beads that clicked as they walked past. How wonderful it would be to have a nun for a teacher instead of Miss Harriet.

"Will you ask Mama and Papa if I can go to the convent with you next fall?" she begged. "Regina won't be there, so I'd be the third one."

"You aren't old enough, dear," said Regina.

23

"But I'll be twelve by then."

"Maudie would be lonesome without you," said Hetty.

Fresh resentment filled Luvvy. Would she be tied to Maudie all her life?

"But Maudie is just a child, and she has Marylou."

"You're still a child too," said Betsey.

A lump rose in Luvvy's throat. She remembered the house she had been building with playing cards. Just as she had laid a card lightly on the last room for a roof, the whole structure had flattened on the carpet. She felt as if that was what had happened to her now.

"Girls, girls!" came a high quavery voice from the bottom of the steps. "Dinner's ready. Mama said for you to come right away."

"All right, Maudie," Betsey called back. "We're coming."

Regina quickly began parting her hair with the silver-edged comb. Hetty straightened the gold medal on her chest. Betsey was already out of the door, because she loved to eat.

"Tell Mama Della I'm coming as soon as I put a bow in my hair," said Regina. "You all go on down so Papa won't get impatient."

Dinner was a Sunday feast even though it was Saturday. The tablecloth, bleached so snowy white by Mrs. Shaw, was almost hidden under great serving dishes of vegetables fresh from the garden, a mountain of whipped potatoes, Martha's best coleslaw, which had a mustardy nip to it, the hot bowl of spoon bread that quivered in the center, and little side dishes of pickles and jellies. But looming above all else was the fat golden chicken, set on a platter before the pile of plates at Papa's place.

When Papa carved the chicken, it was a ritual. First he gingerly tested his thumb against the blade of a knife that was almost a sword. Never quite satisfied, he picked up his own table knife and honed the other against it.

"You'll ruin the silver, Clay," protested Mama.

Then Papa made a rapierlike thrust at the chicken's tail, and fluffy stuffing burst out. A quick slice at each thigh and the legs lay apart on the platter.

"Can I have a drumstick, Papa?" asked Luvvy.

Papa ignored her as he began the delicate operation of cutting paper-thin slices from the breast. With great deliberation he set the carving knife down on its little stand and began serving the heated plates before him.

"I know you like white meat, Della," he said to Mama.

Luvvy finally received her drumstick, and the pieces on the platter diminished quickly, but there was no worry. Two more golden hens waited in the warming oven, one with legs already inelegantly torn off by Pansy to feed Maudie and Marylou.

Martha herself swept in, holding high a platter of steaming beaten biscuits. "Eat them while they're hot," she ordered.

Regina daintily balanced a forkful of fresh peas over her plate. "Papa," she said, "you promised that at dinner you'd tell me what you and Mama Della are giving me for a graduation present."

Papa took a tantalizingly long time to mix melting butter into his spoon bread. "You haven't made any guesses yet," he said.

Regina dropped the peas back on her plate. "Is it a horse for my very own? Luvvy wrote that the bay mare has a new colt."

"No," said Papa, "but all of it has four legs."

"All of it?" asked Regina in bewilderment.

"All of it," repeated Mama. "But they don't move."

"What color is it?" asked Regina. "Brown? A fur coat for next winter? One with little paws hanging on it? Madeline Carr has such a stylish one."

"I don't think you'll want brown," said Mama. "I saw a beautiful green set in Brunswick."

"Green fur!" exclaimed Regina.

"You tell her, Della," decided Papa. "It was your idea."

"It's a new set of bedroom furniture for you to pick out," announced Mama. "Your father and I have decided that you may have your own room now. The one off the back porch. It has such pretty pink wallpaper."

"Oh, Mama Della! Papa! How wonderful!"

Luvvy thought it was wonderful too. Now there would be an empty brass bed in the Girls' room.

"Can I—may I move in with the Girls then?" she asked eagerly. "I'm too big to sleep in the same bedroom with Maudie and Marylou."

"I don't see why you can't," said Mama agreeably. "If they want you."

"Betsey and I would rather be by ourselves," said Hetty. "You know we let you come in whenever you want, Luvvy. All you have to do is knock on the door first."

"Besides," added Betsey, "we can use Regina's old bed for when our friends stay all night. Mary Leary from Williamsport has promised to come for a week this summer."

"But I'd move back with the children when anybody comes for overnight," pleaded Luvvy.

"We like our privacy sometimes," stated Betsey. "You should stay with the Children."

Luvvy leaned over her chicken leg and bit into it savagely to hide her disappointment and her swelling tears.

"Never mind, Luvvy," said Regina kindly. "You may visit me in my new bedroom, and I'll always be home now."

"Perhaps I won't," said Luvvy, with a last desperate effort. "Maybe I'll be going to Frederick next year since I'll be twelve. Please, Papa, may I go to the convent too?"

It seemed this would be the only way that she could become one of the Girls.

"Maybe in a few years," said Papa.

"You'll be old enough then," added Hetty, "and time passes so fast."

Luvvy couldn't agree. Hadn't the morning dragged by like a whole week?

"You'd get homesick," said Mama.

"And have nightmares, with all those white curtains around you," said Betsey. "Every girl sleeps all alone in her own 'curtain,' you know."

Luvvy remembered the rows of cubicles in the dormitories, with each bed and washstand neatly partitioned off by long white curtains. She remembered the Girls' stories of how the curtains were allowed to be left open all night during Commencement Week and how the girls sat up in their beds and ate meringues ordered from Dutrow's confectionery shop.

"We'll talk about it another time," said Papa, helping himself to another piece of chicken.

Papa was usually on her side, but the matter was already settled. There was no hope of her going to the convent with Hetty and Betsey in the fall.

With trembling fingers, Luvvy set her knife and fork

together across her plate. She had suddenly lost her appetite. She didn't even want any Lady Baltimore cake.

Nothing ever seemed to turn out the way you planned.

III

Lord Baltimore and
Lady Calvert

It was a hot dull afternoon. Even the cicadas were chirping from the trees in a halfhearted way. The leaves hung listlessly.

Mama and Regina had driven to Brunswick in the buggy to pick out Regina's bedroom set. And over the protests of the lively colt, Sam had ridden the bay mare to Knoxville to be shod. So Luvvy couldn't even go horseback riding.

Hetty was lying in the hammock, stretched between the aspen and the maple, reading a novel. Betsey was on the porch, reading too. But Luvvy knew that Hetty was enjoying her book more. "I always feel like I'm the beautiful heroine," she said with a dreamy sigh.

Luvvy sat on the porch steps, her elbows on her knees and her chin in her hands. Nothing interesting had gone by on the road. Only the Virts' buggy and the Stonebrakers' wagon. She certainly hadn't thought it would be this way once the Girls were home.

Maudie was the only one who seemed to have any energy. She was making a house among the roots of the aspen. There were great hollows between them, which made the rooms. Now she was busy setting up a table of bark. She broke off the stems of the Queen Anne's lace she had picked at the side of the road and laid the frilly white heads on the bark for doilies—like the ones Regina was crocheting for Mama.

"Do you want to get your dolls and play house with me?" Maudie asked Luvvy.

"You know I don't play dolls anymore."

"Then can I have them?"

"No, Maudie. I'm saving them to give to my own children when I grow up. Like Betsey's saving her big doll."

Maudie returned to setting out rose-petal plates on the lacy doilies. Luvvy jumped up from the steps and leaned over Betsey's shoulder.

"What are you reading?" she asked.

"*Agatha's Hard Sayings*," replied Betsey, without raising her eyes from the print.

"What's it about?"

"A girl in love."

"Would you like to take a walk to the orchard and see the tree where my doves live?" asked Luvvy hopefully.

"Don't bother me now. I want to finish my book before Papa gets home. You know he always gets mad when he sees us reading novels because he thinks they're a waste of time."

Maudie turned from her root house. "I'll go to the orchard with you."

Luvvy ignored Maudie. She stayed behind Betsey, reading aloud some of the words on the page.

Betsey shrugged with vexation. "Don't read over my shoulder, Luvvy. I hate to have anybody do that. Why don't you take Maudie to the orchard?"

"All right, I will if nobody here wants to talk to me."

Maudie's face brightened, and she rose hastily. "I'm ready, Luvvy."

Luvvy immediately regretted her decision. Without another word, she ran through the side gate and toward the apple orchard. Maudie followed, crying, "Wait for me, Luvvy. I can't run so fast."

But Luvvy's pace quickened until she reached the rail fence. A great brown bird had risen on silent wings at her approach. His claws were drawn up into his feathers and his curved beak lowered.

Luvvy was terrified. What if his sharp eyes saw the defenseless doves in their nest? She shook her short skirt at him.

"Shoo! Shoo!" she shouted, as if she were chasing a hen.

Maudie picked up a stone and threw it into the air. "Go away, bad bird." It fell against a fence post.

After a few more lazy glides, the hawk slowly flapped away toward the Harpers Ferry Gap.

Luvvy hurried to the doves' tree. Perhaps the hawk had already killed the feathered twins. She shinnied up the trunk.

"I'll scare the hawk away if he comes back," promised Maudie.

To Luvvy's relief, the two little doves were still safe in the nest, although they looked as if they would soon outgrow it. Their brown feathers were mottled and fluffy.

"They aren't really big enough to take home," Luvvy called down. "I saw their mother feeding them with her beak only yesterday. But I don't dare leave them here because the hawk might come back."

She lifted one dove carefully. Holding it in her hand, she slowly backed along the branch, then slid down the trunk. Her dress didn't matter today. It was just an everyday cotton which she had almost outgrown. But even her Sunday dress wouldn't have mattered.

"Here, Maudie," she said. "You hold this one while I go up after the other. Now don't squeeze her. There! Hold her just like that. I think she's the female."

Luvvy returned for the other bird. When she had

him safely down the tree, she showed him to Maudie. "See, he's a teeny bit bigger. So he must be the male."

"Perhaps they are both the same," suggested Maudie.

"It's never that way. Doves are like the pigeons in the barn. There are always two, a male and a female. Now be careful how you carry her, and don't drop her, crawling through the fence."

"I won't. Aren't you glad you let me come with you, Luvvy, so I can help bring the doves home?"

"Yes, I'm glad you came," admitted Luvvy grudgingly.

"What are you going to name them?"

"I've already named them Lord Baltimore and Lady Calvert."

"Can I help take care of them?"

"Sometimes. But I don't want you fooling with them when I'm not around. You're always into my things."

Back at the house, Luvvy eagerly showed her pets to Betsey, who was still reading her book.

"Look, Betsey!" she cried, holding out her dove. "I've brought Lord Baltimore home because there's a hawk around the orchard. And Maudie has Lady Calvert. Show her, Maudie."

Betsey impatiently raised her eyes from Agatha's problems and looked at the birds.

"They're cute," she admitted. "Now run along and teach them to fly or something."

She became absorbed in the book again.

"Do you want to see them, Hetty?" asked Luvvy.

Hetty turned a page of her novel without raising her eyes. "Some other time, Luvvy. I'm right in the middle of an exciting part."

Luvvy turned away in disappointment.

"Let's go and fix a nest for them," she invited her younger sister. "I've been saving my old Easter basket in the attic."

The basket was woven of green straw and had a huge pink bow on the handle. It was just the right size for the doves. They nestled into the green confetti like two Easter chicks.

Luvvy lifted Lord Baltimore out and held him under her chin. "He feels so soft and tickly," she said. "I'll call him Balty for short. I can't be yelling 'Here, Lord Baltimore. Come down, Lord Baltimore,' when he's flying around."

Maudie took the other dove into her stubby fingers and copied Luvvy. "E-e-eh!" she squealed. Lady Calvert was fluttering her wings, which made her feathers feel doubly ticklish. "She smells like the barn."

"They smell like dusty hay," decided Luvvy. She raised the dove to her cheek, and his little bill scribbled over it. "I bet they're hungry. Little birds want to eat all the time."

"Like us?" asked Maudie.

"Like you, anyway. I'll carry them down to Sam and see what he thinks I should feed them. He must be back from Knoxville by now."

The hired man was their authority on Nature. He knew how to trap muskrats, when to look for the first poke greens, where various birds were most likely to nest, and on the second of February he was the one who brought them the important news that the groundhog had seen his shadow—which was an even more dependable forecast of a late spring than that in the *Farmer's Almanac*.

Valley was back in the barnyard with her colt, so Sam must be nearby.

Luvvy found him in the tack room over the springhouse. His cot and washstand were among the bunches of harness hanging on pegs. He was polishing her saddle with fumbling strokes. Luvvy gave a quick glance at the half-empty bottle sitting at his elbow. Fumes from it and the familiar smell of leather mingled.

Sam's thin sandy hair and straggly moustache made him look as if he were molting. He could have been any age because, although his shoulders were stooped from labor, there was scarcely a wrinkle in his face. He stood unsteadily as he examined Luvvy's doves.

"They're a bit on the young side, Miss Luvvy," he said. Then she knew that he had been drinking from the bottle because in his sober periods he only used the title of "Miss" for the Girls. "Too young for grain yet.

You'll have to make up some pigeon milk for them. Crack some corn fine and soak it in a little milk. You might even cook it a spell on the stove. I'll make a cage out of chicken wire when they get bigger."

Luvvy and Maudie went to the corncrib on one side of the carriage house. Luvvy found a small tin bucket and picked up a yellow ear of corn. She shelled it, twisting off the hard kernels with all her strength. They rattled into the bucket.

Then she trudged up the hill to the big stump on which Martha pounded the dough for beaten biscuits. She used the ax beside it to break the kernels into fine bits. Maudie kept guard to see that nobody was coming, because the well-scoured stump and the axhead were sacred to the biscuit dough.

"Now's the hard part," Luvvy told Maudie. "I don't know if Martha will let me cook the pigeon milk on the stove."

Martha was a tyrant in her kitchen and sometimes wouldn't even allow Mama in it. She was especially prejudiced against children, and she had only consented to cook for the Savages on condition that they would never be left in her care. That was why Pansy walked from Sandy Hook six days a week to mind Maudie and Marylou, as well as do some of the heavier housework.

Good luck was with Luvvy. The kitchen was deserted although the stove was still hot.

Luvvy sent Maudie with a cup to the springhouse to

37

get some milk. While she waited she lifted a lid on the stove and pushed in kindling wood to bring the hot coals to full flame. From time to time she glanced fearfully toward the door, but there was no sign of Martha.

At last the pigeon milk was simmering. Luvvy wondered how long she should let it cook. She was wet with perspiration. Maudie kept lifting her skirt to wipe her face.

"What are you brats doing in my kitchen?" shouted a sharp voice behind them. Luvvy and Maudie jumped.

Martha stood in the doorway, her mousey hair wetly brushed into a tight bun on top of her head.

Luvvy didn't have to wonder how much longer the milk should boil. "I'm making pigeon milk, but it's done now," she said quickly. "We're just leaving."

Martha grabbed a dish towel and flapped it after them. "If I catch you making pigeon milk or rooster milk or any kind of crazy stuff on my clean stove again, I'll tell your father on you. And the next time you young ones fire up my kitchen like a train engine in the middle of a June day, I'll pack my stuff and go back to the mountains."

When they were safe in the hall, Maudie asked, "Do you think she really will?"

"What? Tell Papa or leave?"

"I wish she'd leave, but I hope she won't tell Papa."

"She won't do either." Luvvy spoke from experience. "She never does. Will you get one of Little Mary Spara-

38

grass' spoons and bring it up to the attic? It will be good for feeding the doves."

It took some experimenting to learn how to get the pigeon milk down the doves' throats. Luvvy did most of her practicing on Lord Baltimore. She found that the best way was to spoon some of the mixture into his beak, then gently run her fingertips along the outside of his gullet to force it down. By the time she began feeding Lady Calvert, she had become as expert as a mother dove. Both nestlings seemed satisfied.

"I'll keep them up here for a while," said Luvvy. "When they get bigger, I'll take them out on the roof and let them learn to fly."

Balty thrived on the pigeon milk, but each day Lady Calvert grew more feeble. She lay in the basket with her neck limp and her eyes closed.

Luvvy anxiously carried her down to Sam. "Lady acts sick," she explained. "What can I do to make her well?"

Sam shook his head. "Nothing, Luvvy. She's not going to live. You took her too young."

"But Balty's doing fine. He's so lively he won't stay in the basket."

"He's the one got the strong egg."

"Isn't there something I can do?" pleaded Luvvy. "Give her some medicine or something?"

"No, Luvvy. Only her mother could help her, and she's gave up her nest by now I'm sure."

Luvvy hurried to the orchard to see if the parent birds were still around the peach tree. But the nest was deserted and wind-torn.

The next afternoon while Luvvy was holding the bird in her lap, Lady gave a quick shudder, then grew cool to her touch.

"She's dead," sobbed Luvvy, lifting the limp dove against her cheek.

Maudie laid her head against Luvvy's shoulder. "I'm real sorry, Luvvy. But I'm glad it's Lady and not you. I'd feel a lot worse then."

"Will you come to Lady Calvert's funeral?" Luvvy asked Betsey later. "Maudie and I are going to bury her in the peach orchard under her old nest. We've shrouded her in one of my silk ribbons and put her in my pretty pink writing-paper box."

"I can't," said Betsey. "We're going to the Stone-brakers to play croquet." She looked at Luvvy's tear-stained face and added kindly, "I'm sorry about your dove. You were so fond of her."

But Luvvy and Maudie weren't the only mourners at the funeral. Sam came, although his face was very red and he stumbled from time to time. But he dug a grave under the orchard tree and Luvvy gently laid the box in the hole.

"Seems like we should give her some kind of a send-off, Miss Luvvy," suggested Sam. So he took off his straw hat, bowed his head and said, "You, Who watch the sparrows fall, keep Your eye on this poor little bird. And bless her and Balty and Miss Luvvy and little Maudie here. And me too, of course. Thank You. Amen."

He shoveled the fresh dirt over the box.

"I'll find a big flat rock to cover it good," he said, "so's the foxes don't dig her up."

"It can be her tombstone," decided Luvvy, "and I'll write the name and dates on it."

"And I'll pick some of those daisies over there to put on top," said Maudie.

Luvvy helped her gather them while Sam lurched away for the rock.

Maudie asked, "Will Lady go to heaven?"

"You know birds and animals can't go to heaven," said Luvvy. "They don't have souls like us."

"I'll give her a little piece of my soul," offered Maudie earnestly as she broke off a daisy.

Luvvy had to laugh, although the occasion was so solemn. She put her arm around Maudie's shoulder. "If only you were older, we could have such good times together."

IV

The Canalboat Picnic

"I'll make the potato salad, Mama Della," said Regina, "if you'll bake a couple of pound cakes for the picnic."

"We'll have Martha fry the chicken the night before," decided Mama.

Luvvy heard them through the open window of the sitting room as she was climbing up the maple tree outside. She almost lost her grip on the branch.

Oh, how glorious! It was about time that the Girls had a party. There hadn't been a single dance in the parlor yet. And where would this picnic be? Would they carry everything into the apple orchard and play

42

games among the trees? Or would they all get into the Machine and drive far off to some unusual spot? Whatever they did, it was going to be lovely!

Luvvy lowered herself to the ground and went inside.

"Where's the picnic going to be?" she asked happily.

"What big ears you have, grandma!" exclaimed Regina with a laugh. "We're going to have it on a canalboat between the Weverton and Harpers Ferry locks."

This was more exciting than anything Luvvy could have thought up herself. She began a stiff-legged little dance.

"I've always wanted to ride on a canalboat," she cried. "Every time I go to the lock and watch them put a boat through, I just want to step right on and go to Washington or Cumberland."

Regina looked apologetic. She put her hand on Luvvy's shoulder. "Oh, honey, this picnic is just for the big girls and some of their gentlemen friends. Alec Garrett is coming all the way from Brunswick."

Alec was a friend of Regina and Hetty.

Luvvy's lips tightened. "But you've nearly always taken me on picnics with you."

Mama tried to comfort her. "Maybe Papa will take us for a nice ride in the Machine while the Girls are on the picnic."

Luvvy began to sniffle. "I've always wanted to ride on a canalboat, and I love picnics."

Regina put her arm around Luvvy. "Some other time we'll take you on a canalboat," she said. But Luvvy well knew that "some other time" usually meant never. It was only a phrase to make children bear some disappointment.

She headed for the attic to cry by herself.

She took Balty from his cage and perched him on her shoulder. He was a well-grown bird now, with spots on his wings and a pale pink tinge to his breast. His little black eyes glittered like the glass-headed pins in Mama's sewing basket.

"I don't care if they won't take me," Luvvy told him. "I'll never go anywhere with them again. They're mean. That's because they're my half sisters. And they treat me like I'm their stepsister."

Balty nodded his sleek head as if he agreed. He stretched his neck and pecked at her cheek.

Suddenly there was an angry voice in the lower hall. A door slammed. There was the stamping of feet on the stairs.

Luvvy ran to the landing, with Balty flapping his wings to keep his balance on her shoulder. There was Betsey dragging bedclothing behind her with one hand and clasping a pillow with the other.

"I'll never sleep in the same room with you again!" yelled Betsey to somebody below. "I'm going to move up into the attic by myself."

"You should try to curb your temper, Betsey," came

Hetty's cool voice. "What would the nuns say if they could hear you now?"

"I'll never speak to you again!" shouted Betsey. "And I'm glad Regina *won't* be back at the convent next year. I'll never speak to her again either."

Betsey continued up the stairs. The sheets trailed behind her like the train of a queen's gown.

"What's wrong?" asked Luvvy in a hushed voice. "What did they do to you?"

"They won't let me go on the canalboat picnic," replied Betsey. "They say I'm too young. Well, if I'm that young, I'll just move out of Hetty's room forever."

Luvvy felt a quick sympathy for Betsey. She also felt better about her own disappointment. She was almost happy.

"I'll help you make up the bed in my playroom," she offered. "I'll even sleep in it with you. I'm too big to be in a room with two little children."

Betsey pouted, but she followed Luvvy into the big south room. They began to lay the bottom sheet on the bare springs. Luvvy patted their sharp round outlines.

"It may be uncomfortable at first," she admitted, "but we'll get used to it. I'm used to sitting on it without a sheet even."

Balty flew up on the white enamel head bar and sat there watching them make the bed.

"Hetty's selfish," declared Betsey. "She just wants

everything for herself. Well, now she can have our bed-room all for herself."

"Regina's selfish too," added Luvvy, helping to tuck the top sheet in at the foot.

"They're both selfish," said Betsey.

"And Hetty's bossy."

"Regina's stuck-up because she's so pretty."

"Hetty too, because everybody says how neat she is," said Luvvy.

"They think they're smart because they're the oldest."

"Let's stay together and do things without them," said Luvvy.

She was filled with happiness. It didn't matter about Regina and Hetty. Betsey had accepted her at last.

"Want to come out on the roof with me and watch Balty fly around?" she invited Betsey.

"No, not now," replied Betsey. She sat down on the bed, unmindful of the discomfort. She stared into space, as if Luvvy was not there at all.

"Shall we go horseback riding together?" asked Luvvy. "Valley and Dolly are in the field, but I'll catch them and saddle them for us."

"No," said Betsey. "I don't want to do anything."

"I'll let Balty fly around for a while anyway. I don't like to keep him penned up too much."

Luvvy opened a dormer window and coaxed the dove to it. She stood watching him rise over the treetops in swift, jerky flight. He was soon out of sight. It seemed that every time she let him loose, he flew farther away and stayed longer.

Luvvy began to grow anxious. She climbed out on the roof and walked around, trying to see him in the distance. Twice she was fooled, once by a lone blackbird and again by one of the pigeons from the barn.

"Co-o-o! Co-o-o!" she called.

But still he did not return.

"I've got to go look for Balty," she told Betsey. "Wait and I'll be back real soon."

She went downstairs and outside. She walked between the rows of vegetables in the garden, calling "Co-o-o! Co-o-o!" over and over again.

Sam came to the garden with a hoe over his shoulder. Luvvy ran to him.

"He's gone, Sam," she cried. "Balty usually comes back after a while, but he's been gone so long this time."

The hired man leaned on the hoe. "You've got to learn to give them up when they go, Luvvy," he told her. "Folks and birds. He's gone to be with his own kind, and that's the way it should be. You wouldn't want to be penned up in a cage all your life, and he doesn't neither."

Luvvy nodded despite the lump in her throat. Then she brushed her hand across her eyes and ran back to the attic. At least she had Betsey now.

She raced up the stairs to join her again. She was

47

filled with foreboding when she passed Hetty on the landing. Luvvy went through the open door to see Betsey pulling the sheets from the springs.

"I'm going back to my own room," she explained. "Hetty and I made up."

"Is she going to let you go on the picnic after all?" asked Luvvy with an aching throat.

"No, but Regina's going to let me drive the surrey to Harpers Ferry to pick up some of them when they get off the boat."

"Can I go too?"

"I'd love you to, Luvvy, but there won't be room coming back."

In fresh disappointment and with a new loneliness, Luvvy watched Betsey dragging her bedding down the steps again.

On the day of the picnic, Luvvy made a sudden decision. She would ride horseback down to the lock and watch them board the barge. Then she would ride to Harpers Ferry to see them get off. In places where the road followed alongside the canal, she could watch them eating their picnic lunches.

Betsey would be driving Dolly to the surrey, so Luvvy would have to ride Valley. The mare was skittish when separated from the colt, but he could go along too. That should satisfy Valley.

Saddling the mare was always a job because she was

one of those horses who swell their bellies when the girth is tightened. Luvvy fooled her by giving it a sudden yank when she wasn't expecting it. All the while the colt trotted around them, whinnying nervously.

He had a glossy chestnut coat, with white-blazed face and white stockings. His thick mane and tail were black. Luvvy had named him Sassy.

When she thought the girth secure, she swung into the saddle. Accompanied by the long-legged colt, she started down the road to Weverton.

But no sooner had Luvvy entered the ravine than she noticed the saddle was loose. She didn't want to stop to struggle with the girth. She decided that if she didn't trot, she could keep the saddle balanced in place.

She soon reached Weverton. The village's only importance was that it was the junction for the railroad that ran from Baltimore and Washington to the west and the spur line that went to Hagerstown.

At the canal lock on the other side of the road, some of the older girls and boys had already gathered with picnic baskets and gay chatter. Miss Harriet, Luvvy's teacher, was among them. When she was with the Girls, she always seemed different from the Miss Harriet in the parlor schoolroom. She seemed so much younger and carefree—as if she were as glad as her pupils to get away from the lessons.

Luvvy also recognized Alec Garrett's smart rig among

the others at the hitching rail in front of the one-room post office.

The boat hadn't come yet. Luvvy rode on down toward Knoxville to meet it. The road ran between the railroad and the canal. Luvvy remembered from her Maryland-history lessons that the canal had been started in 1828 by President John Quincy Adams lifting the first spadeful of earth way down near Washington. Slowly the water route had been lengthened until it had reached Cumberland. And now the quaint little boats went its length, carrying coal, flour, grains, and lumber.

The mellow horn of a canalboat signaled the lock-master. Soon Luvvy saw the mule team on the towpath and heard the jingle of their bells. The little boat floated into sight.

Luvvy pulled Valley to a stop and watched the barge go by. It looked like Marylou's little Noah's ark, with the heads of the spare team looking out the curved windows in the bow. The quarters for the crew, covered by a canvas awning, were in the stern.

She returned to the lock, with Sassy prancing along. She could see the surrey coming down the hill to meet the boat.

As Luvvy waited, one of the lock gates was opened and the boat entered through it. As soon as that gate was closed, the other slowly opened. Water from the higher level flowed into the lock, and the boat rose into sight.

By the time it was even with the bank, the surrey

had arrived. Alex Garrett hurried toward it, to meet Regina. The picnickers began hopping aboard, assisted by the young men and the barge captain. Alec Garrett had taken Regina's basket and had his hand under her elbow to help her while Hetty took care of herself.

The gate ahead was completely open now. The mules tugged at the towline, and the boat with its merry passengers moved up the placid canal toward Sandy Hook.

Only Betsey and Luvvy were left behind.

"Hello, Luvvy," called Betsey as she climbed back into the surrey. "You're brave to ride down with the colt."

"I'm going to Harpers Ferry and watch them get off," answered Luvvy. "I'll follow you."

The colt trotted over to Dolly and began nuzzling her harness with curiosity. Suddenly he nipped playfully at her flank. Dolly snorted, flattened her ears, and kicked. Sassy whinnied shrilly and reared. Valley gave an answering whinny, jerked at the bit, and wheeled around. Luvvy felt the right stirrup sink under her foot. She grabbed for Valley's mane, missed it, and plunged to the ground. Luckily her feet came free from the stirrups, and Valley's hind legs jumped over her.

The mare went racing for home, with the saddle swinging under her belly and the colt galloping behind.

Betsey pulled at the reins to bring Dolly under control. "Are you hurt, Luvvy?" she asked as soon as the horse had settled down.

Luvvy rose slowly and dusted off her dress. She saw that her knee was bleeding.

"Just my knee," she said. "I skinned it."

They both looked up the tracks as they heard the long warning whistle of a train coming around the curve. The horse and her colt were headed for the cross-ing in its path.

Betsey screamed and clapped her hands over her mouth. The Baltimore express coiled around the Sandy Hook curve like a giant blacksnake. A long streamer of smoke was unfurling from the smokestack. The horses galloped faster toward the crossing, terrified by the shrill blasts of the warning whistle.

Luvvy covered her eyes with her palms. When she pulled them away she could see that the horses had cleared the crossing just in time.

Betsey was trembling. "Come get in with me, Luvvy," she said unsteadily. "I'll drive you home."

Luvvy climbed into the front seat beside Betsey. She was getting the surrey ride, but not the way she had wanted it.

Betsey pulled the whip from its socket and snapped it over Dolly's back. "We better hurry. Mama Della and the others will be scared to death when Valley gets home with your saddle hanging under her."

Luvvy nursed her knee. She wanted all the sympathy from Betsey that she could get. But it didn't win her the ride to Harpers Ferry.

"I told you there won't be room, Luvvy. And you better go in and let Mama Della fix your knee. It looks awful. When I get back, you can come up to our room, and we'll play cards on my bed."

Luvvy's spirits rose. "We'll play any game you want, Betsey," she said humbly.

Near the pond, they met Sam coming down the road in great bounds, as if he wore fairy-tale boots of many leagues.

"Luvvy!" he shouted when he reached them. "Is she all right?"

He was relieved to see Luvvy was only shaken up. He climbed into the back seat while the surrey was still moving.

"Poor Mrs. Savage is worried sick," he said. "You better whip up Dolly, Miss Betsey. It's bad to trot a horse uphill, but better a mare with broken wind than Mrs. Savage in a faint."

But Mama hadn't fainted. She came hurrying down the road to meet them. Her relief at seeing Luvvy safe in the surrey brought tears and smiles to her face.

Luvvy tried to reassure her about the skinned knee because she was afraid Mama might forbid her ever to ride a horse again.

"It doesn't hurt at all," she claimed. "It really looks worse than it is. Remember the time I went barefoot and stubbed my toe on a rock. That hurt worse."

"We'll go right in the house and clean it with soap

and warm water," said Mama. "But you must never ride that horse again. She's always been skittish."

When the Girls came home later, they too were sorry about the mishap. Regina insisted on putting some peroxide on the knee, which made Luvvy squeal from the stinging.

"Perhaps we should have taken you with us," admitted Hetty.

Regina turned to Mama. "Let's take our supper into the orchard this evening and have another picnic there."

Mama agreed. "I'll tell Martha right away so she won't set the table."

"And perhaps you'll find your dove there," Betsey told Luvvy, "and you can bring him home."

Luvvy was as happy as if they were going on a canalboat.

"Oh, I hope so, Betsey," she exclaimed. "But if I do, I'm not going to bring him home. I want him to be free with the other doves. Maybe he has a mate now. And if he ever has his own baby doves, I'll let them grow up free too."

V

The Buggy Ride

On Sundays the whole family went to Brunswick to attend Mass in the old brick church, St. Francis of Assisi. It was a long tiresome ride this Sunday because the Machine had a flat tire, and they had to take the horse and surrey with two little stools for Luvvy and Maudie.

Regina complained most about the dust and heat.

"But you'll go riding with Alec this afternoon, won't you?" asked Hetty anxiously.

This annoyed Papa. "Why is that young fellow hanging around Regina?" he asked. "I don't think she's serious about him."

56

"But girls get married sometime," said Mama. "You wouldn't want Regina to be an old maid."

Papa snapped the reins across the horse's back. "I certainly don't want her to get married just because everybody else does."

Regina's cheeks were scarlet. "Oh, Papa, Mama Della! Who said anything about marriage? Certainly not Alec. Now let's talk about something else."

After dinner was over, Regina went to her new bedroom to buff her nails and dab some toilet water about her ears and throat.

Luvvy ambled out of the front gate to the hitching rail. It was a long pole that stretched across almost half of the front fence—a reminder of the days when Shady Grove had been a stagecoach stop.

She straddled the rail and pretended to be riding horseback. She wasn't allowed to ride Dolly after the horse had gone on a long trip. And, of course, Valley was still forbidden to her.

The crunch of carriage wheels and clopping of hoofs came up the Weverton road. Luvvy watched until she saw the Garretts' black mare's long neck straining at her collar. Behind rolled the shiny buggy with Alec holding the reins.

Luvvy jumped off the rail and watched his approach. When the horse slowed in front of her, she greeted

57

Alec, then offered, "I'll hold her while you go to get Regina."

Alec laid the reins across the dashboard and leapt down without even touching the step. He was a tall, muscular young man with what the Girls' novels often described as "a lock of raven hair falling across his brow." He pulled off his round straw hat and brushed back the raven lock.

"That's mighty nice of you, Luvvy," he said. "I'll be back soon if Miss Regina is ready."

"She's probably perfuming herself, but I think she'll be right down. She always keeps an eye on the road to see if you're coming." Alec looked pleased. "Where are you all going for a ride?"

"Probably Harpers Ferry, if Miss Regina wishes."

"Oh, I'd love to ride to Harpers Ferry. I'd have to pay toll to cross the bridge if I went there on horseback."

"Perhaps you'd like to join us," invited Alec with more politeness than enthusiasm.

"Indeed I would, thank you," replied Luvvy.

Alec looked gloomy. He slowly made his way to the grilled iron gate and up the brick walk. Luvvy waited impatiently with a tight hold on the bridle. She stroked the horse's face. Horses had such smooth, flat faces—just like the horsehair sofa in the downstairs sitting room.

After what seemed ages, the pair appeared on the

porch and moved down the walk. Luvvy was pleased to see that Regina was wearing her floppy hat with the enormous pink rose on it. She looked like the girl on the cover of the latest *Ladies' Home Journal*, so Luvvy felt that Alec couldn't help falling madly in love with her if he hadn't already.

As soon as they were through the gate, Luvvy let go of the bridle and quickly climbed into the buggy.

"You can't stay there, Luvvy," said Regina. "We're leaving right away."

"I invited her to go," explained Alec glumly.

"She can't," protested Regina. "She looks too untidy for a Sunday ride."

"I'll sit in the middle," said Luvvy. "Then nobody can see me very well."

Regina realized that Luvvy had no intention of being left behind.

Papa came from the house with a section of the Sunday newspaper in his hand.

"Wait a minute," he called.

"I hope he doesn't expect to go too," said Regina.

But that was not Papa's intention.

"As long as you're going for a drive," he said to Alec, "I'd be much obliged if you'd drop some cats along the way. The pesky creatures are overrunning the barn."

Alec's eyes seemed to glaze. "Certainly, Mr. Savage. It would be a pleasure."

"Why, Papa," exclaimed Regina indignantly, "you know we don't want to drop cats on a Sunday drive."

It was the local custom to get rid of cats by collecting them in a sack and dropping them off at a neighbor's farm. As everyone did this, the cats in that part of Maryland led a migrant life, but felt at home in almost any barn.

Alerted by the approach of the Garrett buggy, Sam was already coming up the hill from the barn with a wriggling grain sack in one hand.

"I don't mind dropping the cats," Luvvy assured Papa. "I know where most of them belong anyway."

"And I'm sure that Alec doesn't mind," said Papa.

"Oh, indeed not, Mr. Savage. It will be no trouble at all."

Sam didn't wait for anyone's approval. He stepped between the wheels and set the writhing sack on the floor near Luvvy's feet.

"You be sure to keep the top twisted till you get well away from here," he cautioned. He looked toward Papa. "That's only some of them, but it's all I could catch so far. That's the trouble living on a main road like this. We get all the cats dropped on us."

"Now have a nice ride," said Papa as Alec took Regina by the elbow to help her into the buggy. The young man walked around and climbed into the driver's seat. He backed the horse, then pulled the whip from its socket to spur her speed.

Papa stood waving his newspaper at them. As Luvvy

craned her neck to keep waving back, she could have sworn that he was laughing.

They followed the Sandy Hook road that ran between orchards. The wheels gritted through the dusty ruts, the horse's hoofs rose and fell with a muffled sound, and the cats mewed piteously at their feet.

Luvvy watched the reins raising little tufts of hair on the horse's croup. "Sam says you shouldn't trot a horse uphill," she said to Alec.

"Let Alec do the driving," said Regina.

"I was only trying to be helpful." Luvvy leaned over and cautiously peered into the sack. "I think there are four of them. Oh, I wish Sam had kept the white one. Let's take him back with us."

"We are going to get rid of all the cats," declared Alec grimly, "and at the very next house."

But when they reached the Virts' farm, Mrs. Virts was out in front of the brick house, picking flowers. Luvvy stood up and waved to her.

Regina jerked at her skirt. "Sit down and don't call attention to us."

Luvvy obeyed. "And there's the Millers' house where the striped cat belongs. I love yellow houses. What color house do you want when you get married, Alec?"

Regina's cheeks were as pink as the rose on her hat. "Hush, Luvvy, and don't ask silly questions."

"What's silly about that? Lots of people get married and go to live in their own houses."

Regina quickly pointed ahead. "Look at that pretty bird in the persimmon tree. What kind is it, Luvvy?"

"I don't see any bird in the persimmon tree."

"You didn't look quickly enough. It flew away."

They were now going downgrade, toward the canal and the railroad tracks.

"You shouldn't trot a horse downhill either," said Luvvy. "It makes them springhalted. That's what Sam says."

Alec pulled at the reins and the breeching strap tightened across the horse's thighs as she held back the weight of the buggy. At the foot of the hill, she was brought to a complete halt.

"This is a good place to dump the cats," said Alec. "There is no one around to see us, and they'll quickly find the way to some farm. Will you please hold the reins, Miss Regina?"

Regina's gloved fingers tightened on the leather lines while Alec jumped down. Luvvy passed the mewling sack to him, and he gingerly held it away from his white linen suit. He laid it in the ditch beside the road.

"Open the mouth of it in the direction of the Millers," suggested Luvvy. "That's where the striped one belongs, and the others can go there too."

They drove through Sandy Hook where the road was covered with black cinders. Luvvy waved to everyone she knew. Nearly all the cottages were inhabited by workers on the canal or the railroad.

"Please stop waving, Luvvy," implored Regina. "We don't want everybody in Sandy Hook staring at us."

"But we don't have the cats with us anymore."

"If you'll be a good girl and obey your sister, I'll treat you both to a soda when we get to Harpers Ferry," Alec promised her.

Luvvy always enjoyed crossing the Potomac Bridge. The planks rumbled with such hollow sounds under the horse's hoofs. Below them the river was filled with large gray rocks.

Alec headed his horse down Shenandoah Street while Luvvy warned him to find a shaded spot to tie the horse.

"See the sweat on her flanks," she said. "Sam says that when a horse has had a long pull she shouldn't be stood out in the sun. There's a good place under that sycamore."

They found a cooler spot for themselves in the ice-cream parlor with its marble-topped tables and spindly chairs. Alec treated Luvvy not only to a soda but also to a big bag of hard candy to eat on the way home.

That night was sultry as well as warm. The moon hanging over the Virginia mountains looked like a red-hot skillet. The river moved as sluggishly as molten steel.

Mama had already put Maudie and Marylou to bed in the swing on the upper porch. A pallet on the floor beside it was waiting for Luvvy. The others would stay up half the night on the lower porch, where they were now sitting.

Lightning bugs winked on the lawn. Luvvy was trying to fill a glass jar with them so that she would have a nightlight by her pallet. It was hard to catch a lightning bug. Just as you made a grab for one, its light went out and it vanished. But there was a faint glow in the bottom of her jar.

The cricketlike sounds made by Mama's rocking chair were interrupted by the lonely wail of a train approaching the Weverton crossing.

"Were there many people in Harpers Ferry today?" Mama asked Regina. "The railroad is running special excursion trains from Baltimore since Island Park is so popular."

"I wouldn't know, Mama Della," replied Regina. "I was never so mortified in my life—squeezed in with a child and a sack of cats. And I could see that Alec was frightfully embarrassed."

"We discussed all this at supper," said Mama. "Luvvy has promised not to go driving with Regina and Alec again—no matter how insistent he may be. And Sam will get rid of the rest of the cats."

"Has Alec proposed yet?" asked Hetty. "He's so handsome! I wish he were courting me."

"He surely didn't get a chance today," retorted Regina, "and he is so shy."

"I will not have Alec Garrett marrying Regina for her share in my tool business," declared Papa. His cigar glowed like a huge lightning bug.

Mama said, "That is an unfair way of looking at it, Clay. As Regina realizes, Alec belongs to an old Maryland family, and his father owns a prosperous shoe store. Why, when I took Luvvy in to buy her shoes, there were two customers ahead of us."

"And I certainly won't have my daughter marrying a man for his shoe store," stormed Papa, the light on his cigar making zigzags in the blackness.

Mama reminded him, "Remember that I married you when you owned a thriving tool factory. Do you think I married for money?"

"That was different," argued Papa. "You were twenty-three years old. Regina is only seventeen."

"She'll be eighteen this fall," put in Hetty, "and our mother was eighteen when she married you."

"There is no comparison," stated Papa. "Besides, I have been thinking lately that Regina might like to become a lawyer. That is what I wanted to be, but my father made me go into his business."

"Oh, please be a lawyer, Regina," cried Luvvy from the aspen tree. She had studied Shakespeare with Miss Harriet so she could imagine Regina, a girlish Portia with a big bow on top of her head, declaiming, "The quality of mercy is not strained."

"But I don't want to be a lawyer," protested Regina,

and Luvvy's vision of beauty and justice faded. "I guess I should get married. That's what all my friends are going to do—except Madeline Carr, who's going to be a nun."

"Alec certainly is interested in you," said Mama. "Taking you driving twice a week. I think you should have a little talk with him, Clay, and ask what his intentions are. He will ruin Regina's reputation if he doesn't marry her after all this buggy riding."

Papa stamped on the floor, then rose from his chair. "You know how I feel about all this nonsense," he shouted, "so I refuse to be the accomplice in such a tomfool plot. I'm going up to bed."

Luvvy dropped another lightning bug into the jar, then studied the pale light. Perhaps it would be more romantic to have Regina marry Alec—with the wedding reception on the lawn, under the canopy of green trees and with all the birds singing in chorus.

VI

The Proposal

"Mama, what can I do?" whined Maudie, pushing her finger around in her mouth and plucking at her mother's skirt. "I don't have anything to do."

"Why don't you play with Little Mary Sparagrass?" suggested Mama, deftly mending the sock stretched over a glass egg.

"I'm tired of playing with her."

"Then why don't you take a nice walk to the field and look at the horses?"

"Nobody will go with me."

"Won't Luvvy?"

"She's just lying in the hammock, doing nothing.

67

And she doesn't want to do anything. There's nothing to do."

Mama thought for a few minutes as she wove tiny stitches together. Then she glanced at Maudie. "Tell Luvvy I want to see her. I'll ask her to play with you for a while."

Maudie went through the hall and out the door. "Luvvy," she piped. "Mama wants to see you. She says you have to play with me."

Luvvy soon appeared, her face dark with indignation. "I don't see why I have to play with her, Mama. She's been tagging me all day. I can't even rest in the hammock without her being after me like a mosquito."

Mama kept on darning the sock. "I didn't say you have to play with her, Luvvy. But if you would like to entertain your little sister for a while, I'll let you have the last wallpaper sample book."

"To make a paper-doll bookhouse?" asked Luvvy with a change of expression.

"Yes," answered Mama. "I've really finished with it because I don't think we'll do any repapering this summer. And you can have last year's Sears, Roebuck catalogue."

Luvvy had one more condition to make in exchange for entertaining Maudie. "Will you cook some paste for us? I know Martha won't let us in the kitchen."

"All right, dear. I'll make some right now," said Mama, putting down the sock.

When they needed paste, Mama always boiled flour and water together. But first she found the wallpaper book and the catalogue.

Luvvy enjoyed making paper-doll houses this way. And since she would be doing it for Maudie, it didn't make her seem childish.

She sat on the floor, Maudie squatting close by. She leafed through the bound samples. Each page was a different pattern of wallpaper. Each would be a different room with cutouts of furniture pasted on it.

"Look at this purple with little pink roses and gold loops, Maudie. Wouldn't you like this page for your parlor?"

Maudie nodded and turned a few more pages. "Oo-oh! This beautiful green with gold. Let's have that for Dolly Dingle's bedroom."

"And what about this blue with little arrows. That can be Bobby Bumps' room."

"Will you cut out the furniture, Luvvy? You don't leave pieces of paper on, like I do."

Luvvy turned to the household section of the catalogue and began clipping the pictured pieces she thought suitable for the different rooms. Mama soon returned with the paste in a chipped cup.

Betsey came in with a book in her hand, her finger marking her place. She too became interested in the house. She had taught Luvvy how to make them in wallpaper books.

69

"And why don't you cut out some of the harness horses and paste them on the cover as if they're standing in front, ready to take someone for a drive?" she suggested.

"They never have any legs on them," complained Maudie.

"That's because the company only wants to sell the harness," explained Betsey.

"It can be Bobby Bumps' horse, because he's come to take Dolly Dingle to the Jefferson Rock," said Luvvy. "Just like Alec Garrett took Regina there today."

Hetty joined them and admired the paper-doll house. Then she said to Betsey, "That reminds me. We were going to change our bedroom furniture around. Will you help me now so we can surprise Regina when she gets back?"

Betsey laid her book face down on the little marble-top table, then followed Hetty out.

Luvvy glanced at the book. It must be the one they had been talking about at the supper table the night before—*Maggie Miller*. Since Maggie had found out that she was the granddaughter of the housekeeper instead of the rich Millers' own daughter, could she in all honor marry her sweetheart? The Girls and Mama had refused to tell Betsey because they said it would spoil the book for her.

"I'm tired of fixing the paper dollhouse, Maudie,"

said Luvvy. "You go right ahead, and I'll give you the scissors and the catalogue. I'm going to read for a while."

Maudie was satisfied because she loved to get into paste, and she had a few ideas of her own about furnishing the wallpaper house. She wanted to put a lawn swing in the parlor, and she knew that Luvvy would never agree to that.

Luvvy picked up Betsey's novel and tried to decide where to go so that she wouldn't be disturbed. If she went back to the hammock, Betsey could easily find her and demand the book. Also, Maudie would be running out every minute to show something she had just pasted.

She decided on the parlor because no one ever went there unless it was to entertain special callers. And it was usually cool.

Once settled on the red carpet near the great black piano with its toothy yellow keyboard, she turned to the last pages of the novel so she could find out if the story ended happily. It did, so she began the first chapter.

She had just reached the part where the old housekeeper was exchanging the babies when she heard voices at the hall door.

"Oh, pshaw!" muttered Luvvy. "Mrs. Shaw and all the little Shaws!"

One of the voices outside said, "Wasn't the view from the Rock exquisite?" That was Regina. "Jefferson said that it was worth a trip across the Atlantic."

"And no Little Miss Flypaper or any cats." That was Alec Garrett.

The door opened and Regina saw Luvvy. She looked as annoyed as Luvvy felt. Alec saw Luvvy too. His face fell.

"Luvvy, dear," said Regina, "will you go somewhere else to read? Alec and I would like to talk alone."

"I was here first," retorted Luvvy, turning a page.

She was smarting from Alec's remark. Why had he invited her on the buggy ride if he didn't really want her?

"Oh, don't disturb her," said Alec politely.

Luvvy wondered if he realized she had heard him before.

Regina looked doubtful, but she sat down on the plush loveseat. Alec stiffly lowered himself onto one of the fragile gilt chairs nearby.

"It *was* a lovely ride," said Regina. "Did you like the watercress sandwiches?"

"I've never tasted such good sandwiches."

Luvvy looked up. "Papa hates watercress sandwiches. He says they're just weeds between slices of bread, and that no red-blooded man would touch one."

Alec laughed as if his high collar was cutting off his breath. "He should taste one of your sister's. He might change his mind."

"He did once," responded Luvvy. "That's when he said it."

Alec leaned over. "What is your book about?" he asked.

Luvvy melted a little. "It's about a girl who's in love with a man. And he's in love with her. But she doesn't want to marry him because she's found out that she isn't really the Millers' daughter. The housekeeper changed the babies. Would you marry a girl if she turned out to be somebody else? Like you found out that Regina really belonged to Martha?"

"Luvvy!" exclaimed Regina. "Don't talk so much and read your book."

"But he asked me," said Luvvy in an injured tone, "and Maggie really did marry him in the end."

Regina sat folding her lacy handkerchief into squares and triangles on her lap. Alec leaned forward and began to crack his knuckles. For a few moments there was no sound but that and Marylou's wailing about something in the distance.

Then Alec said, "Would you mind going out to the hitching rail, Luvvy, to be sure my horse hasn't broken loose?"

Luvvy went to the French window that opened like doors.

"She's still there," she assured him. She flopped down on the carpet again.

"How about making some lemonade for us?" suggested Regina. "You can have some of it too."

"There was a lot left over from yesterday. Pansy was going to bring it from the springhouse when you all got back."

"Can't you go to help her?" asked Regina crossly. "I don't think you're reading that book at all. Your eyes don't even move."

Luvvy began rolling her eyes.

Alec squirmed in the gilt chair. "I see by the *Farmer's Almanac* that it's going to be a dry summer."

"I hope it won't rain on the Fourth of July," said Regina. "Will you ride in the Brunswick tournament again?"

"Yes, I've been practicing. Father promised to give me his roan mare if I win."

"Your father is a fine old gentleman," commented Regina.

Luvvy remarked, "I saw him in the store when Mama bought my pumps. They cost three dollars. On sale."

Alec said, "Father is talking about taking me in the store as his partner."

"It's no wonder," said Regina. "You're so intelligent and competent."

Luvvy suddenly pushed the book away.

"Will you and Regina get married then?" she asked.

The room became stifling with the summer heat. Re-

gina's face flamed a bright red. Drops of perspiration broke out on Alec's forehead, and he reached for the handkerchief in his breast pocket.

"If s-she will h-have me," he stuttered as he mopped his forehead.

Luvvy closed her book with a snap and then rose. "That's all I wanted to know. I'll give *Maggie Miller* back to Betsey now."

She scurried out of the parlor to tell everyone that Alec and Regina were engaged.

"They're sitting on the love seat together," Pansy announced with a giggle when she returned from bringing the tray of lemonade to the parlor.

Luvvy was bursting with pride and importance because she had helped to get Regina engaged. Besides, with Regina completely out of the house, Hetty and Betsey might be willing to let her become the third Girl.

But when Alec finally left in his buggy and Regina came slowly up the brick walk to where the whole family was eagerly awaiting her announcement, Luvvy thought that she had never seen Regina look so grief-stricken.

"Papa! Mama Della!" she cried. "I've never been so humiliated in my life." She burst into tears. "That child has ruined everything for Alec and me."

Mama looked as astonished as Luvvy felt. "But aren't you two engaged now?"

76

"Yes," answered Regina between sobs, "but—I have been robbed—of a proper proposal."

"What do you mean?" asked Mama.

"Do you know how I was proposed to?" asked Regina indignantly. "Luvvy asked Alec if he was going to marry me. It was Luvvy who really proposed, not Alec."

"But he is going to marry you, isn't he?" asked Mama.

"That's not the point!" She buried her face in her handkerchief and sobbed bitterly.

"Luvena Savage," scolded Mama, "how could you do such a thing to your sister?"

Luvvy was bewildered. "But everybody wanted Alec to ask Regina to marry him. I was only trying to help."

"Oh, Luvvy," said Hetty. "They are supposed to be alone when the man proposes, and he goes down on his knee."

Betsey glared at her. "When will you ever grow up and get some sense?"

Luvvy began to cry. But Papa put his arm around her shoulders to comfort her. He furiously turned upon the others.

"I don't know why you're all picking on Luvvy," he shouted. "You wanted to get Alec and Regina engaged, didn't you?" He shook his finger at Mama. "And *you* even wanted me to do the proposing for him. And now that Luvvy did it for me, you're all mad at her. I tell you, I will never understand women—not even with a house full of them."

Everyone looked crestfallen, and Regina stopped crying. She rolled her handkerchief into a damp ball.

"I hope you are *all* satisfied," she murmured. Then she stalked to her room.

"Maybe she didn't want Alec to propose," said Luvvy in astonishment.

"How ridiculous!" exclaimed Hetty. "Any girl would be thrilled to have Alec propose to her."

VII

The Tournament

"*I can't imagine* what's keeping Mr. Savage so late," fretted Mama. "He must have missed the four-fifteen from Hagerstown. But he's never been this late before."

"Maybe the train got in a wreck," Pansy suggested as she helped Mama rearrange the supper plates for at least the fourth time. "Remember that awful one near Martinsburg? Killed ten passengers and the fireman."

"Hush, Pansy!" ordered Mama. "It's probably a late shipment that kept him at the factory."

Martha stuck her head through the little serving window in the wall between the kitchen and the dining room. "Everything's going to get cold as the crocks in the springhouse," she complained. "And the pork chops all frizzled a'ready."

"Maybe we better have Sam hitch up the buggy and go to the depot to meet him," said Mama.

"I'll tell Sam," offered Luvvy, "and I'll go with him."

Surely Mr. Garver, the stationmaster at the depot, would know if there had been a wreck on the Hagerstown line. He was kept in touch with everything by that dit-dot, dit-dot telegraph machine in his office.

But as she went flying down the hill she saw Papa hurrying up the Weverton road.

"What's wrong, Papa?" she asked breathlessly. "Was there a wreck?"

Papa took her by the hand. "Nothing like that, Luvvy. Only a little extra business I had to attend to."

It wasn't until he had the family around him that he explained the business.

"A circus went bankrupt out of Williamsport," he told them.

"What did that have to do with the train?" asked Mama.

"Nothing at all. But they sold off some of the animals. I went to the auction."

"Oh, Papa!" cried Luvvy excitedly. "Did you buy some kind of circus animal?"

"A lion or tiger?" asked Maudie with big eyes.

"Not quite a wild animal," answered Papa. "I bought a fine horse for practically nothing."

Mama looked bewildered. "But we already have Dolly and Valley. Or perhaps we need another workhorse now that the harvest is coming on?"

"I don't know if this horse could be trained to a plow. He's never been in regular harness. Belonged to some bareback rider who eloped with a fellow in town."

Luvvy began clapping her hands in her excitement. "Like that white horse May Wirth rode when you took me to the circus in Washington?"

"Maybe a little heavier," said Papa. "But a fine piece of horseflesh."

"But what will we do with a circus horse that has never been broken to harness?" Mama asked.

"He only cost me a hundred dollars," said Papa apologetically. "I couldn't turn down such a bargain. I would have lost money."

"Clay Savage," said Mama indignantly. "I don't believe you have much sense. A useless horse to eat its head off."

"Where is he?" Luvvy asked. "Did he come on the train with you?"

Papa winked at the Girls. "How else would I get him here? He's so well trained that he sat on the seat across from me until a lady got on. Then he politely gave her his seat and went into the smoking car to have a cigar."

"You're teasing me, Papa," accused Luvvy. "Please tell me where he is."

"That's why I'm late," explained Papa. "After the

auction I went down to the Williamsport wharf and arranged with one of the canalboat men to bring him down the towpath with the mules."

"What's the horse's name?" asked Luvvy.

"Pepper. And that's exactly his color. Handsome iron-gray. They expect to get here Friday morning."

Waiting for Friday morning. And it was only Tuesday. Always waiting.

After what seemed a week, it dawned. Luvvy walked to the Weverton lock with Sam. She planned to ride the circus horse home, although Sam would lead him with the halter in his hand.

"I'm going to learn to do tricks on Pepper," she informed Sam. "I used to want to be a writer when I grow up. But now I've decided to be a circus rider instead."

"One sounds as hard as the other to me, Luvvy," said Sam. He could neither write nor read, but he knew how hard it was to be a good rider.

They crossed the little footbridge over the sluiceway and went to the bank of the canal. There was no boat in sight, so Luvvy entertained herself by crossing the plank bridge made by the top of the gates when they were closed. She walked impatiently up and down the towpath. She looked up the canal and tried to imagine Cumberland, where many of the barges were loaded with coal from the mines. She turned downriver and remembered the stately white buildings of Washington, where the canal ended.

At last the faint echo of a horn came to her ears. She hurried back before the gates should open and leave her stranded between the canal and the river.

"Why don't they hurry?" she asked Sam.

"Can't hurry a mule," he informed her. "They only move about two miles an hour."

At last she could see the team driven by a young boy. There were only the two mules, hitched tandem. The number on the blunt prow of the boat was Fifteen, but where was Pepper?

In her impatience, the scene seemed as motionless as a painting. Then she could make out a great gray horse tethered on the deck.

The lockkeeper had already begun closing the lower moss-grown gates to raise the water level in the lock.

"They'll change teams while they wait to go through," said Luvvy knowingly. "Do you think they'll take Pepper off then?"

But before the mule teams were changed on the opposite side, the boat was pushed against the bank on which Luvvy and Sam waited.

The hired man gripped the halter tighter as the fall-board was laid to shore. Then he went aboard and joined the crew members. They talked a few moments, then untied the handsome iron-gray horse with flowing

83

white mane and tail. Although he was a huge Percheron, he pranced gracefully across the fall-board as if the circus band were playing and his hoofs cushioned by sawdust.

"Oh, he's beautiful, Sam!" cried Luvvy. "He's very handsome. He's—he's *majestic*."

Sam boosted her up on the broad iron-gray back.

"He's so big and flat I feel like I'm doing the split," she remarked. "It'll be easy to stand up. I'll try when we get on the road."

"Now take care, Luvvy," cautioned Sam. "I don't want you getting hurt while you're with me. Your pa'll say I've been tippling sure. If you want to break your neck, do it by yourself."

But Luvvy paid no attention to him. As soon as they were back on the cindery road, she cautiously braced her arms against the horse's withers and lifted herself to her knees. Slowly she rose to her feet.

Pepper's back made a splendid platform.

"It's easy when he's walking," she said. "When I get used to it this way, I'll have him trot."

"Not while I'm leading him," declared Sam.

She swayed slightly to the rhythm of the horse's powerful muscles. Then she lowered herself and sat sideways with both feet dangling.

"I wish girls could ride in the tournaments," she said. "I'd take him to Brunswick and ride him myself. The only trouble is that even if girls could ride, the

Fourth of July is day after tomorrow, so I couldn't enter this year."

"Don't know if he'd go fast enough anyhow," said Sam. "Tournament rules are the horse has to charge seventy-five yards in eight seconds."

"I'll find out how fast he can go when I get a bridle on him," promised Luvvy.

When they reached home, Luvvy was disappointed because Mama and the Girls' weren't as interested in Pepper as she and Sam. Maudie and Marylou were even afraid of him.

That evening Luvvy performed on the horse's back for Papa.

"Oh, Clay," cried Mama, "I wish you hadn't bought that horse. Luvvy will kill herself."

"No, she won't," declared Papa confidently. "She's a born bareback rider if there ever was one."

It was the tradition to drive to the Fourth of July picnic in the surrey even though the Machine was in working order. To make enough room, Luvvy had to ride horseback, with Maudie straddled behind her. That was the way they always went to Miss Harriet's house during the school year, but Luvvy felt humiliated because she thought that she now belonged in the surrey with the Girls.

Alec Garrett would have called for Regina in his buggy if he hadn't been riding in the tournament after the picnic. But he had to get his roan mare there and take care of her until time for the big event of the day.

He did join them where the marshmallow-white table-cloth was spread over the trampled grass, and ate more than his share of the ham sandwiches, according to Luv-vy's secret count. But she couldn't begrudge them to him because he looked so handsome in his orange blouse and white duck trousers. He was entered as the Knight of Old Potomac.

"When is the tournament going to start?" Maudie kept asking between bites of the chicken. Marylou was happy feeding scraps of food to the ants of the nearby hill.

Before they had finished eating, Alec's father and mother came from their own picnic spot to invite Regina to stay over in Brunswick for supper with them. They promised to drive her home in time to dress for the ball. Luvvy decided that they were the ideal parents for Alec.

The tournament field had already been staked out. Posts with great crossarms were set in a line. Flags flew over the red-white-and-blue bunting decorating them. Already knights were in practice—tilting at the rings suspended from the arches.

Old Mr. Condon, one of the outstanding citizens of Brunswick, was consulting with other riders in their bright varicolored blouses and checking names and teams on a dog-eared piece of paper because he was Lord of the Tourney.

He opened the contest by announcing, "And now, ladie-e-es and gentlemen, you are about to witness the oldest sporting event in America—one which goes all the way back to sixteen hundred and thirty-four in our own great state."

After what seemed an endless flow of words about knighthood, patriotism, and the Fourth of July, the Lord of the Tourney ended with the appeal, "And I would charge everyone present to be his own knight and make just complaint to the Baltimore & Ohio Railroad for blocking the Knoxville and Weverton crossings for such long periods."

This brought the loudest applause.

Soon the tournament was under way.

First, there was a parade of the knights, with the spectators clapping and whistling for those of their choice.

"Knight of Old Potomac!"

Alec rode the roan mare slowly through the arches, his lance at rest.

Then the electrifying command came from the Lord. "Charge, Sir Knight!"

The horse was wheeled around, then urged to a full gallop. The Knight of Old Potomac rose in the stirrups and set his lance. As the roan thundered down the course, Alec, in Luvvy's eyes, was no longer a clerk in his father's store. He was a knight of old in shining armor, with a white plume fluttering from his helmet.

Hetty shared her vision. She gripped Regina's arm.

"Oh, isn't he wonderful!" she declared. "He rides just like one of King Arthur's knights. I know he will win."

"I hope so," said Regina. "This tournament means so much to him."

One horseman after another galloped down the field. Knight of the Chesapeake. Knight of the Shenandoah. There was even a Knight of Loudoun, who had crossed the river from Virginia wearing spurs on his boots and carrying a lance that had been in his family for nearly a hundred years.

Luvvy was spellbound by the thunder of the horses' hoofs and the red flare of their nostrils. Dust clouds rose from the broken turf. Bright blouses ballooned and snapped in the wind.

When each knight had had his turn, most carrying off all three rings, smaller circlets were set in the arches. This time Luvvy couldn't bear to watch Alec. She felt that her heart was pounding to the roan's hoofs. She hid her face in her hands. She heard *clink, thud, thud, thud, clink, thud*— She opened her eyes in time to see the Knight of Old Potomac spear the third ring.

Luvvy began clapping wildly.

"Luvvy!" exclaimed Regina. "Stop putting on such

an exhibition! Do you want everyone staring at me?"

"Aren't you proud to be Alec's fiancée?" asked Hetty. "I wouldn't mind them staring at *me*."

"The Knight of Loudoun will probably spear all of them too," put in Betsey.

Her prediction came true. But a number of riders missed one or two rings.

So it went on until the last round when circlets no larger then Mama's gold wedding ring had been captured or missed by the competing knights. They presented their lances to the Lord, and he pulled off the rings. It did not take long to figure out who had won the most points.

"Hurrah! Three cheers for the Knight of Old Potomac!"

Alec's father shouted the loudest, and his mother clapped the longest. Regina gently tapped her palms together. It didn't seem modest to applaud her own victory since she would be crowned Queen of Love and Beauty.

Luvvy forced her way through the crowd to where Alec now stood rubbing the sweat from his horse.

"I'm so proud of you," she cried. "Now you've won the horse too. Please, please, may I get up in the saddle?"

Alec lifted her before she had a chance to put her foot into the stirrup.

"She's pretty overheated," he stated. "If you'll just walk her around slowly, she'll cool off without a blanket."

Luvvy proudly guided the horse around the field. She hoped that everyone knew that she was the sister of the girl the Knight of Old Potomac was going to marry.

She felt giddy with reflected glory. She only wished that all these people could see her performing on Pepper. That was the next best thing to spearing rings at a tournament.

Maybe they could see her, although Pepper was home in the field. To be sure, the mare's back was narrow, but Luvvy was already adept at keeping her balance when standing. And Alec's saddle was broad.

She proudly pulled her feet out of the stirrups and raised them to the saddle. She rose to her full height. She could easily have plucked the rings from the bars.

Some bystanders were already noticing her prowess. Clapping and cheering rose from the tournament field again. The audience grew larger as news of the exhibition spread.

Luvvy began to bow and throw kisses, as she had seen May Wirth do under the same circumstances. Her last bow turned out to be directed at Regina, who was standing with the elder Garretts and frantically beckoning to Luvvy. From Regina's face, her half sister

could tell that she was not filled with pride or admiration.

"Get down from that horse immediately!" Regina commanded Luvvy with anger only controlled by the presence of her future in-laws. "Aren't you ashamed? Making a spectacle of yourself before everybody in Brunswick!"

Luvvy dismounted and led the horse back to Alec. Her head was bowed in humiliation. It was Regina who had made a spectacle of her, with such a public scolding. And right in front of Alec's parents.

Without a word she returned to the surrey where Mama and the other two Girls were packing the remains of the picnic.

Regina wasn't far behind her.

"Mama Della!" she exclaimed. "I don't know what gets into Luvvy. Showing off before a crowd of strangers!"

"What was she doing?" asked Mama.

"Standing up on Alec's horse and putting on a show. I can't imagine what Mr. and Mrs. Garrett must think of our family."

"And you don't even have your riding knickers on," said Mama. "People must have been able to see your drawers."

"But they're new and have lace on the bottom," protested Luvvy.

Papa didn't look shocked. "Probably the Garretts

thought the same thing of our family as they did of their own when Alec won the tournament," he said.

But what Papa said had little consolation for Luvvy because Hetty and Betsey sided with Regina.

Luvvy had little more to say until they had finished putting the picnic things back into the surrey. Since Papa seemed to be her champion, she asked him, "May I go to the dance with the Girls tonight?"

"You're too young for dances, Luvvy," Mama put in quickly. "There won't be any children there."

"But I'm not a child anymore. I'll be twelve, week after next. And Betsey is only fourteen."

"But I don't get to dance," explained Betsey. "I just sit with the chaperones and watch. And I get sleepy toward the end."

Regina herself began to feel sorry for Luvvy. "I'll bring my crown home to show you," she promised. "I guess it really didn't matter about your standing on the horse. After all, you're only a little girl, so the Garretts probably thought it was cute."

Since Regina was staying with the Garretts, there was room for Maudie in the surrey. But she insisted on riding back behind Luvvy.

"Poor Luvvy," she said. "She looks so sad, and she needs me."

Luvvy felt that Maudie's company was the last thing she needed under the circumstances, but she grudgingly agreed to take her on Dolly.

"I'm just Cinderella," she complained as they rode home, "and they're my mean stepsisters. And Mama acts like she's their mother instead of ours."

"I wish I was your Fairy Godmother, Luvvy," said Maudie. "I'd wave my wand, and you'd be wearing Regina's purple-and-gold party dress. And you'd be so pretty that Alec would crown *you* the Queen instead of her."

VIII

Twelfth Birthday

"*If Mary Leary comes next week,* she'll be here for my birthday, won't she?" asked Luvvy as if there could be any doubt about it. She was particularly fond of Mary.

"Now don't be hinting about your birthday," cautioned Betsey, "as if you expect a present from her." Mary was Betsey's special friend because she was closest to her age.

"You know I won't," said Luvvy indignantly. "I'm too old for that. I wish I could have a party this year, but I don't know who I could invite."

Luvvy didn't know any of the children who lived in the nearby villages or on the farms. Most of the time she felt no need for friends outside her family. Thanksgiving, Christmas, and Easter were family holidays. But a birthday was an occasion to share with friends.

"Since Mary will be here, we can ask the Stonebraker girls," suggested Regina. "We haven't invited them to anything since we went to their tea."

"And Miss Harriet?" asked Luvvy.

"Yes," said Regina. "We wouldn't want to invite the Stonebrakers unless we asked Harriet too."

"That makes five guests and you all and me," Luvvy counted on her fingers. "Nine of us."

Maudie looked worried. "Won't I get to come to your birthday party, Luvvy?" she asked anxiously. "I won't talk and I'll eat polite."

"Of course you'll get to be at the party," Luvvy assured her. "But you're not a guest. You're my little sister, and this is going to be a grown-up party. I'll be *twelve* years old, you know."

Maudie nodded. "You're always talking about it."

Imagine having a birthday party with grown-up girls for guests, instead of children! Luvvy decided to watch her own manners carefully and not backslide into any childish ways.

The preparations for Mary Leary's arrival began days in advance. The Girls had been busy, cleaning the house and adding special touches to their room. When Luvvy offered to help, they gave her and Maudie the ignominious task of gouging the weeds from the bricks of the front walk. Armed with a small paring knife, Luvvy did her best, although it was the chore she hated most.

"When that is finished," said Regina, "you can help Pansy shoo the flies out of the dining room. Marylou is always letting them in."

Chasing the flies was more entertaining than digging weeds from the walk. Armed with branches full of maple leaves, Pansy and Luvvy went to the far side of the room. Maudie was stationed at the door. On signal from Pansy, they began furiously beating the air with the branches. The swarm of flies was herded toward the door.

"Open it now!" yelled Pansy. "Here they come a-flying."

Maudie gleefully opened the door in time for the flies to be driven outside, then quickly shut it against their return.

They had two more drives to dispel the insects which had escaped the swishing leaves thus far. Then Pansy began swatting at the few elusive ones left.

Marylou came to the screen door and opened it half-way. She stood there hesitantly with a twig from the weeping willow hanging from her hand.

"I want to play too," she said, slowly fanning the door back and forth.

Luvvy made one leap at her and yanked her inside. The door slammed wearily shut. "You get away from that door, or we'll be playing with flies all day, and Mary Leary won't come here."

Marylou began to cry, and Pansy consolingly swept her into her apron. Luvvy made her getaway to the parlor to see if she couldn't do something with the Girls.

There were endless tasks until the very day of Mary's arrival.

"Can I go to the depot with you to meet her?" Luvvy asked Betsey.

She received the old answer. "There won't be room in the surrey because Mary will have her suitcase and everything."

But at the last minute they decided to make room for her. It all began when the surrey wasn't brought to the front gate.

"What's the matter with Sam?" asked Regina. "He surely should have Dolly hitched by now."

"Maybe he's gone on another toot," said Martha grumpily.

Pansy contradicted her. "Sam's gone to Sandy Hook to line up some more hands for gathering in the hay," she said, "and the horses are out in the pasture."

"But surely he was told we needed the surrey to meet the Hagerstown train," declared Regina. "Didn't you tell him, Hetty?"

"No," answered Hetty. "I thought you told him."

"I didn't because I thought Mama Della would."

"I don't even know what time the train is arriving,"

said Mama. "And I thought your father would tell him."

"Did Papa?" Betsey asked Luvvy.

"I don't know," replied Luvvy. "He probably thought you Girls had."

"That's the trouble with such a large family," said Mama. "Everyone expects someone else to attend to things."

Regina began to smile at Luvvy. "You're the only one who can catch Dolly when she's out in the field," she said. "If you'll get her for us, we'll let you go along to meet Mary."

When the horses were loose, they would run away from anyone who entered the pasture. But Sam had taught Luvvy how to catch them without having to chase all over the field. She had kept this a secret from everyone else because it sometimes gained her a favor such as this.

Luvvy ran down the hill to the carriage shed, then peeped through the drooping branches of the great willow to see that no one was spying on her from the house. She pulled a bridle off a peg, then selected an especially large ear of corn from the granary.

When Luvvy entered the pasture, she hid the bridle behind her with one hand and held out the corn in the other.

The horses raised their heads from the lush grass and eyed her suspiciously. Luvvy slowly walked toward

Dolly, talking to her in a low voice. At first the mare shied away, her ears flattened. But the sight of the corn was too tempting. She changed her mind and stalked toward it. As soon as Dolly's teeth clamped on the ear, Luvvy grabbed her by the forelock. After such capture, a horse never resisted further. She was given time to finish the corn, then the bit was pushed into her mouth. It was that easy to catch a horse in the pasture, but nobody in the family had thought of it.

Luvvy even harnessed Dolly herself, although the collar with all the attached straps was heavy to lift and buckle. But she had to call Betsey to hold up the shafts of the surrey so she could back Dolly between them.

They heard the whistle of the Hagerstown train coming through the creek ravine before they even started down the hill.

"Hurry, hurry!" Regina urged Luvvy, who was doing the driving. "Mary will think we have forgotten about her coming."

"If she could have seen us doing all that cleaning, she wouldn't," said Luvvy. But for once she disregarded Sam's warning about a horse trotting downhill and snapped the whip lightly over Dolly's back.

The train was already standing on the Hagerstown track, its locomotive puffing and steaming as if worn out by the trip.

Mary Leary came around the depot, waving wildly.

She made great bounds across the main tracks, her suitcase thumping the rails and a hatbox bouncing in the air.

There were squeals and giggles as Mary dropped her luggage and tried to hug everybody at once. Then she straightened her sailor hat and tossed the suitcase into the back of the surrey with one mighty swoop of her angular arm.

"Maybe I've brought too many clothes," she said, "but it's such a relief to get out of those serge dresses and black sateen aprons they make us wear at the convent."

Luvvy squeezed in back with the hatbox so Betsey could drive home with Mary beside her.

Hetty took a long look at the crowded surrey and decided to walk. "I will get my dress all rumpled if I get in too," she said.

Luvvy almost offered to join her, but then smugly settled back on the seat beside Regina. After all, she was the one who had caught the horse in the pasture, so she deserved a ride both ways.

For most of the afternoon, Luvvy hung around Betsey and Mary.

"What have you been doing with yourself all year?" Mary asked.

"We have a new circus horse, and I'm learning to do tricks on him," answered Luvvy. "When I grow up,

I'm going to be a bareback rider like May Wirth."

Betsey laughed. "When we were home for Christmas, you were going to be a naturalist like Ernest Seton Thompson and live in the north woods with a pet wolf."

Luvvy blushed to think she had ever had such a foolish ambition. "I was only a child then, and I got that book, *Wild Animals I Have Known*, for a present." She turned to Mary. "You should have been here Christmas. Papa dressed up like Santa Claus, and Marylou was so afraid of him when he came to the door Christmas Eve that she bawled and bawled."

"He had to leave and let Mama Della give out the presents," added Betsey.

Luvvy continued. "The girls and men from Sandy Hook dress up in costumes and masks and go around to the different farms between Christmas and New Year's. They sing songs and bang on pans outside. Then Mama invites them all in for eggnog and cake. I knew Pansy right away, even though she had burnt cork smeared all over her face, because she was wearing an old sunbonnet."

"I think it's an old English custom," explained Betsey. She added, "Of course you remember we didn't get home for Easter because we had the measles and the nuns put us up in the infirmary for all the holidays."

Mary grinned. "I guess they couldn't make you sit on

the punishment bench up there. Remember the time you got mad and broke the tennis racket?"

Luvvy sat down on the floor close to their feet. She loved to hear them talk about convent days.

"I think it's silly to have to play baseball with a tennis racket," declared Betsey. "And I think it's ridiculous for Mother Mary Austin to say that playing with a bat would be unladylike."

"You must have sat on the bench for two hours, Bets, before you gave in and thanked Sister Mary Agnes for punishing you. I'll never forget the look on your face—as if you didn't mean it at all."

"That's adding insult to injury," declared Betsey. "Having to thank the nun in charge."

But Mary Leary laughed heartily, as if it had all been quite a gay romp.

"Tell more," Luvvy begged. "Tell me about Commencement Week."

"The nuns let us do things then that we're forbidden the rest of the year," said Betsey.

"Like sitting up half the night with our curtains pulled back—like a house party."

"And being allowed to send out to Dutrow's for meringues and getting to eat them in bed."

Luvvy had heard about the meringues, but the Girls weren't able to bring any home because they were great balls of ice cream in a Nabisco-like shell.

"I want to go to the convent this fall," said Luvvy to Mary. "Don't you think the Girls should ask Papa to let me?"

Mary couldn't understand such a wish. "You're lucky to be able to stay home. Summer is the best part of our year, isn't it, Bets?"

"Luvvy doesn't know how lucky she is," agreed Betsey.

But to Luvvy even the punishment bench sounded like an exciting challenge.

In a few days she would be twelve years old. Perhaps Papa and the Girls would change their minds about her going to the convent.

On the morning of her birthday, she awoke excited and happy. Something wonderful was going to happen today. She rubbed her sleepy eyes, then came wide awake from the shock of realizing that she was *really* twelve years old.

She jumped out of bed and ran to the big mirror over the bureau. As she looked into it she assumed a serious expression. Yes, she did look older. When she had combed and braided her hair, she wound the braids around her head. Even Betsey said that it made her look grown-up.

The Girls gave her their present early so that she could wear it for the party. It was a party dress of pink lawn which they had made themselves. Luvvy could tell Betsy's big loose stitches from Hetty's dainty ones, scarcely visible to the naked eye.

"Thank you, Girls," said Luvvy politely, trying to feel really grateful for a childish-looking dress with a waist that dropped almost to the hips and a short ruffled skirt. Maybe those times they had locked her out of their rooms had been when they were working on the dress.

Mary Leary gave her a present, even though Luvvy had not hinted once. It was also handmade—an embroidered silk case for hair ribbons. And there were five long ribbons of different colors in it.

Mama and Papa wouldn't give their gift until the party. For the first time in her life, Luvvy had no idea what it might be.

Making the ice cream helped pass the time, although not in the most enjoyable manner. They had to take turns at the freezer for twenty minutes each, with Regina doing the timing. Now and then Mama would drop more salt over the cracked ice.

"Why can't I turn awhile?" begged Maudie. "I want to help make Luvvy's ice cream."

"No, Maudie, you're not strong enough," said Mama.

"You ought to be glad you don't have to," said Luvvy. "It keeps turning harder and harder as the custard freezes."

At last the afternoon arrived. Luvvy was in her pink-lawn dress with one of Mary's ribbons tied around her head with a rosette bow.

When the Stonebraker girls drove up with Miss Harriet in their surrey, the party officially began.

The Stonebraker girls looked alike. All three of them had pale blue eyes, pale blonde hair, and pale complexions. They were dressed in pastels—Louise in pale blue, Elizabeth in pale yellow, and Jane in pale green. Luvvy thought that they looked like angels. She liked them so much better than the present they brought. It was an assortment of handkerchiefs purchased at Kaplan's in Brunswick. Luvvy already had enough handkerchiefs for ten winters of the grippe.

Miss Harriet gave her a volume of *Hans Brinker*. "I remember you once mentioned you'd like to read it because you loved ice-skating," she said.

"Every winter when I skate on the pond," Luvvy told her, "I play a game with myself. Each time I start out, I'm a different President of the United States. I try to see how many times he can get around the pond before one of my skates comes loose. John Adams skated around eight times once, but Buchanan fell down near the cattails. The ice is always rough there."

The big girls were more than willing to play games on the lawn. They seemed to enjoy Prisoner's Base and I Spy as much as she did. They even argued over the games, which was a sure sign of interest. Of course

Maudie had to be included, and she made a pest of herself because she was always breaking the rules.

Mama and Papa sat on the porch in their Sunday clothes, watching. Then Mama slipped away to bring out a medium-sized package.

"Happy birthday, Luvvy!" she exclaimed. "Here's a gift from Papa and me."

Luvvy eagerly tore the package open. It was a Kodak camera!

"Mama! Papa! Thank you a million times. I never would have guessed." She kissed them in turn.

She had to be patient while Papa pulled out the bellows, then inserted a roll of film. Not satisfied yet, he gave Luvvy instructions on how to use the camera. "And be sure to turn to the next number after you've snapped a picture. Now if you'll all line up, I'll take the first picture of the birthday party."

A picture of herself with all the big girls—twelve years old!

"I'll have it to remember today," cried Luvvy. "The most wonderful day of my life."

"You have lots of most wonderful days, don't you, Luvvy?" asked Maudie.

"But today is special," declared Luvvy as she sidled close to Betsey for the picture.

"One—two—three," Papa counted.

Click! The important scene had been recorded for posterity.

They were on the lawn, eating the ice cream. Luvvy forgot what long and hard work had made it.

"Now what shall we play?" she asked, setting down her empty dish.

"We've finished playing with you, Luvvy," said Regina. "Now I'm going to take the girls to the upstairs porch." She beamed at the grown-up guests. "I learned a new game called Bridge, and I'll teach it to you. It's so much more interesting than Five Hundred."

"Will you teach me too?" asked Luvvy eagerly. "I love card games."

"Only four people can play," explained Regina. "With eight of us, we have exactly two tables. I'll teach you some other time."

Luvvy followed them up the stairs, with Maudie not far behind. "I can sit and talk to you anyway."

"No, no," remonstrated Regina. "You can't talk and bother people when they're playing Bridge. They have to concentrate."

"I'll play Slapjack with you, Luvvy," offered Maudie.

"You can't play it here," said Regina. "It's too noisy, and we must have our minds on our cards. We've helped you celebrate your birthday, Luvvy, so why don't you be a good child and go play downstairs with Maudie?"

Luvvy disconsolately descended the stairs. The birthday party that had started out so wonderfully was ending in this dull, disappointing way. The Girls didn't think twelve was grown-up. They had only been humoring her by taking part in the games on the lawn—the way she would now humor Maudie by playing Slap-jack with her.

IX

Sam

The Girls had gone off again and left Luvvy behind. This time it was to go bathing in the river across from the canal locks.

"Please take me with you," Luvvy had begged. "I love the water."

The Girls were searching through bureau drawers to get old cotton dresses to wear into the river.

"The Potomac is dangerous," said Regina. "You always go in too deep, and we don't want to be responsible for you."

"I promise I won't go out far," insisted Luvvy. "I'll just wade at the edge."

"The rocks are slippery and there are deep holes in

places," added Hetty. "Remember the little boy who drowned near Sandy Hook last summer?"

"But he was in a canoe with his father."

"They weren't out far," put in Betsey, "and the currents are treacherous even near the shore."

So they had driven off without her.

In a mood to wade anyway, Luvvy suggested to Maudie, "Let's go barefoot down to the pond and try to catch some fish. Martha is in the garden gathering peas so we can get a big sieve from the kitchen."

They unbuttoned their slippers and left them with their socks on the front porch. They scampered down the road with the dust spurting between their toes and the dry weeds tickling their ankles.

"Remember the time we caught all those toads at the pond and penned them in the springhouse?" asked Maudie.

Luvvy made a face. "And we thought we'd have fried frogs' legs for weeks. Then Sam told us they were toads that had come to the water to spawn because it was spring. That's why the pond was full of those clumps that looked like tapioca."

"And nobody would drink the milk from the springhouse but you and me."

"I don't know why they were so persnickety. The crocks were all covered," Luvvy added. "But Martha kept saying the toads had been jumping over them— and she called it hoptoad milk."

"But we got those tadpoles later on. Maybe we can catch some tadpoles today."

"It's too late. They've dropped their tails and gone to live on land."

Since the pond was in the horses' summer pasture, it surprised Luvvy to see that the gate was wide open.

"Sam must have taken the horses to the barnyard," she guessed, closing the gate behind them from force of habit.

They arrived just in time to see a muskrat swimming across the pond. He made an arrow-shaped wave as he nosed through the water.

"Muskrats hardly ever come out in the daytime," Luvvy informed Maudie. "They go around all night and sleep during the day."

"Maybe that one is walking in his sleep," suggested Maudie.

They giggled.

The two girls sat on the bank for a few minutes, with their toes wriggling in the cool water. They watched a bright dragonfly zigzag across the surface.

"That's a devil's darning needle," said Luvvy. "Pansy says they'll sew your mouth shut if they can. But Sam says that's fiddle-faddle. Let's try to catch some fish now. Be careful when you step in and stay near the shore."

Maudie clapped her hand over her mouth when the dragonfly darted close to them because she wasn't sure whether Pansy or Sam was right.

Luvvy took first turn with the sieve. She daringly waded out, her feet sinking into the muddy bottom. When she was up to her knees, she stooped over and swept the sieve back and forth under the surface. All she caught was some pondweed and a snail.

"When can I try?" whined Maudie. "Isn't it my turn yet?"

Luvvy finally gave her the sieve. "But stay where you are. It's dangerous to come out far."

Maudie scooped mostly mud and waterlogged sticks.

After two more turns, Luvvy looked down and gave a sharp cry. "Ugh! A sucker on my leg." She wrinkled her nose with disgust as she pulled the slimy leech loose. "Let's not fish anymore. Maybe there aren't even any fish in here."

They went back through the tall sedges and returned to the road, climbing over the gate this time.

At the low plank bridge that crossed the stream flowing from the pond, Luvvy stopped. You hardly noticed the bridge when riding in a buggy, but knew it was there because for a few seconds the horse's hoofs made hollow sounds, followed by a deep rumble of the wheels.

Luvvy stepped off the bridge into the clump of jewelweed and foxtail that bordered the stream.

"I'm writing a story about this bridge," she announced importantly. "I'm going to send it to that children's page they have in the *Baltimore Sun* on Sundays."

"Will you read it to me?" asked Maudie.

"After I finish it. But first I want Betsey to read it to see that my spelling and punctuation are all right."

"What happens on the bridge?"

"Nothing happens *on* it. Everything is under it—like *Alice in Wonderland*. Right under the bridge is a big hole like the one she fell down. Only it's a long sloping tunnel. You can walk to the bottom."

"What's down there?" asked Maudie with wide eyes. "Goblins?"

"No, the tunnel leads to the town of all the creatures that live in the pond—the muskrats and frogs and turtles. The road goes past their back doors." Luvvy stooped and peered under the bridge. "I can see the candles burning in the windows, and there's Mrs. Muskrat crossing to Mrs. Turtle's door to borrow some roots to make root beer."

"Let me come down and see too," cried Maudie, squatting closer to the edge.

"No, you can't. That would spoil it all for you because you'd only see a lot of rocks and weeds. I'm the only one who can see the tunnel and where it leads to."

"Can't I try to see it?"

"No, because as long as you don't look, it will be easier for you to believe my story when I read it to you."

Maudie heard a sound. She turned and looked down the road.

She pointed. "There's Dolly by herself without any buggy or anybody."

Luvvy jumped back on the bridge. "She's loose. I wonder how—the open gate! The other horses must be out on the road too."

She quickly plucked a handful of grass and went to meet Dolly.

The mare stopped and regarded her warily. Luvvy stretched her arm out more invitingly. Dolly came slowly to it, with ears turned forward. A clump of grass in hand seemed more attractive than low weeds for which she had to stoop.

Tangling her fingers in Dolly's mane, Luvvy tried to urge her to walk up the road faster.

"We'll have to tell Sam right away," she said. "You run ahead and see if he's in the tack room. Dolly is so pokey."

Maudie ran as fast as she could, spurred by the importance of the message.

But when Luvvy got to the barnyard gate with Dolly, Maudie came scurrying back to her without Sam.

"He's asleep, and there's an empty bottle beside him. Is he tooting again?"

Luvvy confirmed Maudie's suspicion when she peeped through the tack-room door herself. She took Maudie's hand solemnly.

"We'll have to tell Mama that the horses are loose," she said, "but promise me you won't say a word about Sam. We don't want to get him into trouble."

"I promise," declared Maudie.

Mama and Martha were appalled to hear that the horses were out.

"I'll walk up the road toward Sandy Hook to see if any of them have gone that way," said Mama. "Luvvy, you run down to the barn and find Sam. Have him go down the road for them."

"He can't go after the horses," said Maudie. "He's—"

Luvvy jerked her by the arm. "Come, Maudie! Let's go to the barn, and if we can't find Sam, we'll go down the road."

She made Maudie run all the way until they were out of the house. "We'll have to find the horses ourselves and drive them back," she said, breaking off a switch from an alder bush. "Now if we see them, don't go running up and scare them away. We'll cut across the field and get on the other side of them."

They reached the ravine, without any sight of the animals. Instead, they saw Chris Meador from Weverton bounding toward them, the loose soles of his shoes flapping through the dust.

At sight of the girls, he began waving his arms madly.

"Go tell your ma your big gray horse got hit by the

Baltimore Express," he panted. "He's a-laying down on the tracks."

Luvvy was stunned. It was as if the black locomotive had suddenly struck her. For a moment her tongue was paralyzed.

Then she cried, "Pepper! Hit by a train! Is—is he hurt much?"

"Dead as a doornail. Killed right off. Probably didn't know what hit him."

"I'll go see." Luvvy started to run down the road, but Chris barred the way.

"No, you don't," he declared roughly. "It's no sight for a child. You go back home and tell your ma. And tell her the other horses have been hustled into the Stonebrakers' barnyard."

Luvvy turned quickly so that Chris couldn't see the tears that were beginning to stream down her cheeks. He had called her a child, but she didn't want him to see her weeping like one.

Maudie followed in Luvvy's dust.

"Poor Luvvy!" she sympathized. "Now you won't get to be a circus rider."

Maudie's sympathy made Luvvy cry harder. "It—it—isn't that," she blubbered. "Poor Pepper!"

"Don't cry Luvvy. He's probably in heaven with Lady Baltimore."

"Why couldn't it have been Dolly or one of the

118

workhorses? Or even the colt. Why did it have to be Pepper?"

"Maybe because he's the only one who got on the tracks," reasoned Maudie.

Mama was as upset as Luvvy. She too burst into tears.

Then the Girls arrived home in a great hubbub of horror and excitement.

"At first I couldn't believe it was our horse," declared Hetty.

"Mr. Stonebraker is having his man haul Pepper into the woods. Then Papa can have him buried somewhere. But how did the horses get out?"

"The pasture gate was open when Luvvy and I went to the pond," said Maudie. Seeing Luvvy's frown, she thought it was for another reason. "But *we* didn't do it. Luvvy even shut it after us."

"Where's Sam?" asked Mama impatiently. "Hasn't anyone found him?"

"I haven't seen him all day," said Martha. "He's on a toot for sure."

"Your father will have to deal with him when he gets home," said Mama to the Girls.

Her words chilled Luvvy.

When Papa finally did come, walking up the path from the barn instead of through the front gate, Luvvy knew that he had dealt with Sam.

119

"I've given him his walking papers," declared Papa sternly. "He admitted he didn't half know what he was doing when he drove the horses to pasture. I've had my fill of his tippling. This is the final straw. That horse was worth hundreds more than I paid for him."

"You mean Sam's leaving—forever?" asked Luvvy desperately. "Right away?"

"Right away and forever," pronounced Papa, in a tone that showed there could be no change in his decision. Then he shook his head regretfully. "Too bad! You couldn't ask for a better worker when he's sober."

Luvvy slipped away from the perturbed group and dashed down the path to the barn.

She hesitated at the tack-room door, then knocked lightly. There was no sound until Sam appeared at the door. His eyes were bloodshot, and his moustache seemed to droop more than ever.

"Sorry, Luvvy," he said humbly. "Never meant to leave that gate open. Worse thing is, it was your special horse. Awful sorry."

Luvvy rubbed her eyes. "I'm sorry too, Sam. Sorriest about you. I'll miss you terribly." He had already stuffed his few belongings into an old suitcase. "Where'll you go now, Sam?" she asked.

"Wherever the first freight out is headed," he answered. "That's the way I came and that's the way I'm a-going."

120

He went down the path, still a trifle unsteadily.

"I'll walk with you, Sam, and see you off," said Luvvy.

"That's sure nice of you. Better than I deserve."

They tramped silently for many minutes. Luvvy had to take quick half-steps to keep up with his uneven stride. There was something troubling her, and she wanted to ask Sam about it. But she wondered if she dared. Since this would be her last chance, she finally dared.

"Why do you drink so much from that bottle, Sam?" she asked.

The man looked ashamed. "I don't rightly know. Seems I'm alone so much, with nobody to talk to and nothing much to do."

Luvvy had a surprised feeling of guilt. She recalled that members of the family often joined Martha in the kitchen in the evening. But no one had ever bothered to keep Sam company down in the tackroom.

Sam's tongue loosened. "Seems you can't stop once you get started. Always losing jobs for me. I wish I'd known it before I took my first drink."

They were coming out of the ravine and saw that one of the freight trains was blocking the crossing in the manner that was such a nuisance to the people who drove on the roads.

Sam made an effort at cheerfulness. "See! There's my

own private car waiting for me. Just like I was a millionaire. And looks like I'm going west. Maybe I'll go all the way to Californy and get a job on a ranch."

Luvvy wished that the freight train wasn't already waiting. "You'll write to me sometimes, won't you, Sam? Just a postcard if you're real busy—and tell me how things are going with you."

"Now, Luvvy, you know I can't read or write. But I'll be thinking of you. Years and years from now, I'll be thinking about you and Shady Grove."

"I'll be thinking about you too, Sam."

"Just think of the good things when you do. Not about Pepper and the times I was tippling. Remember how I built a cage for Balty and how I always kept your saddle polished so good. Things like that. It's no use to think about the bad—only hurts you inside."

"I will, Sam. I promise I'll only think about the good things."

They stood close to the cindery bank until the engine whistle blew a shrill blast. Then Sam began climbing the iron ladder to the top of an empty coal car.

The cars ahead, one by one, jerked into motion with a bump, bump, bump at each coupling. The coal car began to move over the crossing. All the others followed without any more bumping.

Sam was on his way west.

Luvvy waved long after he was out of sight, until

122

there were only the men in the caboose to return her wave.

Then she slowly walked homeward, kicking the dust into the yellow goldenrod blooming in the ditches.

X

Maudie

Luvvy and Maudie leaned on the fence rails watching the horses in the pasture. The usually calm animals raced back and forth across the grass and nipped playfully at each other's flanks and withers. The colt frolicked with them, kicking his heels like a child enjoying the antics of his elders.

Maudie licked at the lump of sugar in her hand.

"When are you going to teach me to ride, Luvvy?" she whined. "You said you would sometime. I always have to sit behind you, and I want to be in the saddle all by myself."

Luvvy scowled at her. "Stop eating that sugar, Maudie, or there won't be any left for a horse. You

125

know you have to learn to ride bareback before Mama will let you sit in a saddle by yourself."

"Why?"

"Because that's the way I had to do it. Mama was afraid I'd get thrown from a saddle and dragged to death if my foot caught in the stirrup. So I used to come out here and ride the horses in the pasture. You'll have to do the same. That's why I brought you here today."

Maudie watched the colt frisking with the other horses. "I want to feed Sassy my sugar and ride him."

"You can't. He isn't broken in yet."

"But he's more my size."

"That has nothing to do with it. Pepper was the biggest of all, but he was the safest."

"When will they come over and eat our sugar?"

"When they get tired of playing. They'll be steadier then too. I'm the only one who can ride them without a saddle or bridle when they're cutting up in the field."

Finally the horses quieted down. The workhorses began to graze with fresh appetites. Dolly, with head raised as rigidly as the statue of a general's mount, stood in the middle of the field.

Valley was the first to notice the children. She switched her tail, whickered, and began to approach them. Her colt followed with arched neck and tail.

Luvvy held out the lump of sugar in invitation.

"You can feed her yours after I give her mine," she

told Maudie. "And be sure to hold your hand out flat so she won't bite your fingers along with the sugar."

Valley greedily held out her velvety nose.

"I'll get her against the fence, then you jump on her back real quick," said Luvvy. "And get a good hold on her mane."

Maudie climbed expectantly to the top rail. The colt, having no success at pushing his mother away from Luvvy's hand, moved toward Maudie. He nibbled at her fist.

The little girl lost interest in Luvvy's efforts to maneuver Valley close to the fence. She opened her hand with the fingers bent backward as far as they would go.

Sassy snatched the lump rudely. As he savored it, he wheeled around until his back was just below Maudie. It was such a small back. Just the right size for Maudie's first attempt.

Without saying a word to Luvvy, she quickly straddled the colt's back and grabbed for his fluffy mane.

Sassy gave a terrified whinny and rose on his hind legs. Terrified herself at this unexpected move, Maudie threw her arms around his neck. She could hear Luvvy screaming, "Get off! Get off!" But it was too late to do anything but hold on as tightly as she could.

The colt started across the field, screaming and kicking. Maudie was thrown to the ground. As she started to rise, the colt's hind hoof caught her on the head. She slumped into the grass and lay still.

"Maudie! Maudie!" shrieked Luvvy, running to her. "Are you hurt, Maudie?"

She dropped to the ground and lifted Maudie in her arms. The child slowly opened her eyes. She rubbed her forehead in a dazed way.

"I'm all right, Luvvy. I'm just kind of dizzy." She pulled herself to her feet with Luvvy's help. "I don't think I want to learn to ride today."

Seeing that Maudie seemed all right, Luvvy's mood changed from anxiety to indignation. "I told you to leave the colt alone," she scolded. "If you're not going to listen to me, I'll never, never teach you to ride."

Luvvy decided that Maudie's unusual silence all the way back to the house was caused by penitence.

Mama was upset when they told her about Maudie's fall from the colt.

"And don't blame me because I told her not to," concluded Luvvy. "She never listens to me."

"It wasn't Luvvy's fault," Maudie defended her sister.

Mama felt the bump on Maudie's head, then she ran the back of her hand over her forehead to see that there was no fever.

"I'll put a cold pack on your forehead," she said. "Luvvy, will you run down to the springhouse and get some of the fresh water?" She turned to Maudie again. "You see that riding horses can be very dangerous. You must wait until you're older to get on a horse all by yourself."

"I don't think I want to ride at all," said Maudie meekly.

That evening she didn't want any supper. "There's an ache in my head," she said. "I think I'll go to bed."

Papa didn't even sit down at the supper table. "I'm going to start up the Machine and go to Harpers Ferry to get Dr. Ransome," he said.

The very appearance of the old doctor's kindly face behind the rimless spectacles and trim gray moustache usually made a patient feel better immediately.

Dr. Ransome took Maudie's temperature, looked at her tongue, and left some white pills for her.

"Perhaps she will be better by morning," he said. "I'll stop in early, on my way to see a patient in Knoxville. But if there's any change during the night, don't hesitate to send for me."

Maudie was worse the next day. She didn't get out of bed. She moaned from time to time and complained of the slightest noise. "It makes my head hurt when you hum," she said, although Mama's humming at household tasks was one of her cheery ways which the children liked best.

"You'd better move in with the Girls for the time being," Mama told Luvvy. "I'll put Marylou in our bedroom so Maudie can have quiet."

"I'll sleep in Luvvy's bed, Mama Della, so you can get some sleep tonight," said Regina. "I'm a light sleeper so I'll wake up if Maudie wants anything."

"Thank you, Regina," Mama said, "but I want to be with Maudie."

Marylou began to howl. "I want Mama."

"You see," said Regina. "Marylou may fret for you during the night, and that would only bother Maudie."

Mama gave in. "At least I'll be in the next room."

Hetty and Betsey welcomed Luvvy to their sacred domain. Betsey pulled out a bureau drawer and began emptying it.

"You can put most of your things in here," she said, "and I'll squeeze the dresses together in the wardrobe chest so there'll be room for your Sunday dress."

Before she went for her clothing, Luvvy moved around the room as if to make herself more familiar with each object which would now be associated with her.

She lifted the toilet articles on the bureau, one by one. Her comb and brush would join them. She ran her hand across the mantelpiece and stopped to gaze at the little framed portrait placed in the exact middle. It was of a young woman with Regina's face in an old-fashioned gown.

Was Elizabeth Russell prettier than Mama? thought Luvvy jealously. Did Papa love her more? But it was really impossible to compare the two women because they were so different. Papa must never have compared them either. He had loved Mama and the Girls' mother equally but in different ways. As she loved Maudie and Marylou and the Girls.

Betsey's voice broke into her thoughts. "You'd better get your things now because the drawer is ready."

"I won't bring too much," said Luvvy, turning away from the mantel. "Maudie will soon be well." But she hoped that wouldn't make any difference and that she would be allowed to stay. She arranged her belongings as neatly as possible so the Girls would find no complaint.

Then she sat down on the bed that was to be hers at last and cupped her cheeks with her hands.

So many times she had dreamed of sharing this room with Hetty and Betsey. Now it had become a reality, but not in the way she wanted it. She would never have wished harm to Maudie. Nothing ever turned out the way you planned it.

Dr. Ransome stopped by twice a day. After one of his calls, Mama went to Maudie's bedside with forced cheer in her voice.

"How would you like to go to the hospital in Hagerstown, Maudie?" she asked. "We'll drive you there in the Machine. Papa will go real slow over the bumps so it won't hurt your head."

Maudie began to cry softly. "I don't want to go

away. I want to stay here with you all." She pulled herself up on her elbows with an effort. "I'm beginning to feel better. My head hardly hurts at all."

Since she seemed improved, Luvvy was allowed in for a short visit. She sat down carefully on the edge of the bed so as not to shake Maudie.

"I'm sorry I got on the colt's back, Luvvy," said Maudie. "I should have listened to you. But he looked so little, and I was really afraid to get up high on Valley all by myself."

"That's all right, Maudie," conceded Luvvy. "I don't always listen to what I'm told. Remember the time I climbed up in the aspen tree after Mama told me not to? And I fell out, and could have broken my arm or leg, she said."

"But you didn't hurt your head, did you?"

"I was just lucky. I'm writing a story about you and the way you fell off Sassy."

Maudie's pale face flushed with pleasure. "Are you? Will you read it to me?"

"I can't because it isn't finished, but I'll tell it to you. In the story your name is Caroline. Don't you think that's a pretty name?"

"I guess so, but I like Geraldine better."

"Geraldine doesn't sound like a Southern name—but if that's what you want. You're a little Southern girl, you know, and it's during the Civil War. You've been riding your pony in the woods. I'll make it a pony since

132

you're scared of big horses. You overhear some of the Yankees saying they're going to burn down your house. So you gallop home as fast as you can to warn everybody. But your horse stumbles and throws you into a ditch. And you're unconscious when they carry you home."

"Then how can I tell them the Yankees are going to burn down the house?"

Luvvy frowned. "That's what I'm having trouble with because I want Caroline—I mean Geraldine— to be sick and unconscious for a long time so it will be more exciting."

This problem of plotting didn't seem to worry Maudie. Something else bothered her. "What happens to Geraldine? Will she get well again?" she asked anxiously.

"Of course she gets well in the end. Don't you always get well after you've had chicken pox or a stomachache?"

Maudie looked relieved. She lay back and closed her eyes. "I'm real tired now, Luvvy, so you can go and finish writing the story."

Luvvy tried to make herself useful to the Girls so they would want her to stay on with them when Maudie became well.

That night when a bat got into the room through the fireplace chimney, she had a chance to make herself indispensable.

Pansy said that when bats got into your hair you never could get them out again. That was why Hetty and Betsey were squealing under the covers.

They had sensed the swishing swoops of the bat and seen his shadowy figure in the moonlight that came through the windows.

"I'll get rid of him," Luvvy bravely announced, although she was quaking inwardly.

If the bat got into her long hair, she'd have to cut it all off. She would look a fright and wouldn't dare go anywhere for ages.

She slid out of her bed and made a dash for the commode. She grabbed a towel and wrapped it around her head. Then, crawling on the floor to avoid the bat, Luvvy made for the nearest window. She raised herself long enough to remove the screen, then dropped to the floor again.

All the while Hetty and Betsey cowered in bed, almost smothering in the sheets they'd pulled over their heads.

The bat made a last glide over them, then disappeared through the open window.

"He's gone," announced Luvvy, adjusting the screen again. "It's a good thing you had me here with you tonight."

The room quieted down once again. Luvvy had a few moments to enjoy her triumph before she fell asleep.

But during the night she had a strange dream. The house was full of bats. She could hear excited voices and footsteps racing up and down steps.

She heard Regina call, "Papa has gone for Dr. Ransome. They should be here any minute. Will you come help us, Hetty?"

The dream seemed so real that when Luvvy woke up next morning, she still felt frightened and shaken. She looked toward the other beds. Hetty's was empty, but Betsey was swaddled in her sheets with her eyes closed and her mouth open.

Noiselessly, Luvvy stepped onto the floor in her bare feet.

She was more sure than ever that she really had heard the commotion during the night. Could Maudie be worse? She would go to her room and find out.

Luvvy crossed the hall and went through the spare bedroom. Regina's door was closed, so she continued to the hall in the other wing.

As she neared her parents' room, she heard strange sounds inside. Dry, rasping sounds like somebody sawing wood. She tiptoed to the door and quietly turned the knob so she could peep in.

Papa was bowed in the chair beside the bed, with his hands over his face. His shoulders were shaking with each deep, sawing sound. Papa was crying!

Luvvy began to tremble. She had never seen a man

cry. It was especially terrible to see Papa in such an unguarded moment. It could mean only one thing. Maudie was dead.

She had a panicky desire to run away from the awful weeping and the reason for it. She wanted to hide from anyone who would tell her that Maudie was dead. As long as she didn't hear for sure, there was the chance that she was still alive.

Luvvy made her getaway up the attic steps and into her playroom. She crawled out of the window onto the roof. No one would think to look for her there.

She squatted on the black shingles, with her bare toes curled inside her long nightgown. Then she dropped her head between her knees and tightly encircled them with her arms.

So many times she had been impatient and mean with Maudie. She had even scolded her for getting on the colt. And how she had complained about Maudie always tagging her around!

Luvvy began to sob herself—softly so no one would hear her and bring her the bad news.

Then when she felt as if she couldn't go on living with such grief and remorse, she remembered Sam's words when he had left. "Just think of the good things. . . . It's no use to think about the bad—only hurts you inside."

She made herself recall the kind things she had done

137

for Maudie—like cutting out paper dolls when she really wanted to do something else, or letting her tag along so much of the time.

For a long while Luvvy sat on the roof, thinking of the good things. When she finally made peace with her conscience, she stretched her arms and legs to ease their cramps. She climbed through the window again and began walking slowly down the attic steps. She was ready to have someone tell her that Maudie had died during the night.

XI

The Thunderstorm

After Maudie's funeral the house seemed emptier than ever. Everyone still went around on tiptoe and talked in low whispers. But it was no longer because of Maudie.

Mama was in bed. She wasn't really sick, they said.

"She's given in to her grief," said Papa sadly. "If we could only get her out of that bed, she'd be all right."

Luvvy was as worried as Papa. First Maudie and now Mama. It was too much to bear.

Regina took over complete care of Mama. She carried trays, temptingly set with the company plates and silver.

"Run and pick a red rose to lay on it," she once said

to Luvvy. "That will look pretty, to match the straw-berry jam."

And another time she baked the special pound cake that Mama usually liked so well. But the food was almost always returned on the tray.

From time to time Luvvy would go to the bedroom, where the blind was pulled so low you could no longer see that the corners of the room were rounded, making it look like the inside of a drum.

"The threshing machine is cutting the hay, Mama," Luvvy might say. "If you get up and look out the window in Marylou's room, you can see it."

Or, "They're loading the hay in the barn now, Mama. Will you come down with me to watch them?"

The response was always the same. Mama moved under the cover, but turned her face away so all that could be seen was her long black braid.

"Some other time, Luvvy."

The Girls made no suggestion that Luvvy move back into the bedroom with Marylou, but there was little to cheer her.

Dr. Ransome's visits had begun again, but he never left medicine. There didn't seem to be any kind of pills for what ailed Mama.

One day Luvvy followed Regina to the bedroom door. She shamelessly bent her ear to the keyhole.

After all, Mama was her real mother. Why should Regina be the one who sat by her bedside and tried to comfort her? And how was Mama really coming along? Regina always put on such a cheery face for the rest of the family—like Dr. Ransome. Would Mama really get well again?

She heard Regina's voice. "You heard what the doctor said, Mama Della. You'll become an invalid if you don't get out of this bed soon. You still have us, and we need you so much. And who will take care of the new baby if you don't get well again?"

Luvvy caught her breath. Mama must be expecting another baby! A wave of happiness swept over her. A new baby to take Maudie's place! No! No other child could do that. Not any more than Mama could take Elizabeth Russell's place. But maybe it would be the boy that Papa had always wanted. A little brother!

Not long after, Regina came down with a radiant smile on her face. "Mama Della is getting dressed," she announced. "Now don't anybody act surprised when she comes down. Just act natural."

It was really hard not to act surprised when Mama came walking down the steps, all dressed, with her hair in a neat coil at the nape of her neck.

"I must see how dinner is coming along," she said to Luvvy with a smile, "and I think I'll stir up an angel food cake if there are enough eggs. We haven't had one for a long time."

She began to hum as she walked toward the kitchen. In a few days, it didn't seem that Mama had ever been absent from the family table. But Papa must have remembered. He must have wanted to make sure that she wouldn't become an invalid.

"I'm going to take you to Hagerstown with me tomorrow," he announced at supper, "and we'll do the town. Have dinner at the best restaurant and go to the moving pictures in the afternoon. And how about picking out a new hat?"

"Oh, please get a yellow one with a great big bird on it like the one we saw in the magazine," begged Luvvy.

"But tomorrow is Pansy's day off," said Mama, although she looked pleased by Papa's invitation. "Perhaps we should go day after tomorrow."

"Surely the Girls can take care of Marylou," declared Papa. "And day after tomorrow I might not be in the mood. And maybe all the yellow hats with birds will be sold."

It didn't take too much argument to make Mama give in.

If I were Mama, thought Luvvy, I'd be so excited I wouldn't be able to sleep tonight.

But Mama looked quite fresh and energetic the next morning as she prepared for the trip.

"Tell Martha to be sure to cook enough food for the harvest hands," she instructed Regina. "You know how they can eat. Close all the windows if it should rain. And, Luvvy, you help entertain your little sister."

After the commotion of seeing Mama and Papa off

in the Machine, the Girls went up to their rooms to sort their clothing.

"Miss Luly Violet will soon be here to do the sewing," said Hetty, "so we better see what we'll need."

"I should have a new sateen apron," said Betsey. "Mine is so shiny. Aren't you lucky, Regina? You can have a new party dress made, instead of school clothes."

Luvvy didn't think that Regina was so lucky. She wished she could be having some dresses and aprons made for the convent, but the idea seemed hopeless now.

Betsey opened her drawer and began to throw skirts and blouses on her bed in a disorderly heap.

"If you're going to get a new party dress, will you give me your purple one?" Luvvy asked Regina. "I think it's so beautiful; it's really a *gown*."

"You know it's too old for you, Luvvy. You'd look like the girls from Sandy Hook when they masquerade at Christmastime. And when you grow up, you'll want a brand-new gown for parties."

"No, I won't. I want yours. You'll save it for me, won't you? You won't throw it away?"

Regina laughed. "Of course not. I promise to keep it for you."

Shouts from the road drew Luvvy to the window.

"It's the Stonebrakers on their hay wagon," she said.

The Girls dropped everything and went down to greet them.

"We're going on a ride back in the mountains," said Louise. "Come along."

"We'd love to go," cried Betsey. "We haven't been on a hayride yet this summer."

"No, we can't," Regina reminded her. "Pansy isn't here to watch Marylou. Martha won't do anything like that, you know."

"You and Betsey go," suggested Hetty. "I'll stay."

"No," said Regina, "we won't go without you. If all of us can't go, none of us should."

Since Regina was the eldest, her word was law.

"Then can't I go in your place?" begged Luvvy. "I love hayrides."

Elizabeth Stonebraker had an idea. "Why don't you give Martha a quarter to watch Marylou? I know she'd do it for that. Then Luvvy could go too, since she invited us to her birthday party."

"Oh, please, please, Regina," Luvvy begged. "I'll ask her."

Regina was thinking this over. Then Marylou grabbed Luvvy tightly by the hand. "I don't want to stay with Martha. I want Luvvy."

Sharp memory of another voice pierced Luvvy's ear. *"But I want to be with you, Luvvy."*

She tried to deafen it. "But Martha would be nice to you, Marylou. She'd probably take you in the kitchen with her and let you eat all the cookies you want."

Marylou's grip tightened. "I want to be with you."

Luvvy didn't really feel strong enough to make the sacrifice. It took all her willpower to say, "I'll stay with Marylou, Girls. You go on the hayride."

Regina couldn't understand. "But you were so eager to go with us. Marylou will be all right with Martha as soon as we are gone."

Marylou began to cry.

Luvvy knew that there was no way out. "No, I'll stay with her. I was just fooling about wanting to go. The hay is so stickery it makes me itch, and it's so dusty it makes me sneeze."

Luvvy watched them leave, in bitter disappointment. She wanted to run after them yelling, "Wait for me! I do want to go." But Marylou's tight moist hand held her back.

"Will you take me for a walk?" she asked.

"Where to?"

"I want to see the horsies."

"All right. I haven't been to the pasture since—in a long time."

They stopped to watch the men storing the hay in the barn. Sharp claws were lowered by a rope. They bit into the wagon, raising a great pile of hay. Then a pulley carried them along a rod in the barn. The hay was dropped onto the steadily growing stack below.

"We'd better shake a leg," called Chris Meador to

a man from Knoxville. "Looks like a storm's a-coming."

It was beginning to grow darker as clouds gathered over the Potomac.

"Will it thunder and lightning?" asked Marylou fearfully.

Luvvy studied the sky. "Not for a while. We'll have time to look at the horses. But we mustn't stay too long."

They walked out on the road and went over the bridge that hid the tunnel to the homes of the pond creatures.

Luvvy and Marylou leaned against the gate and looked at the horses grazing on the hill.

"You won't always have fresh grass," called Luvvy. "They're putting your dry food into the barn for the winter."

The colt pointed his ears questioningly. He slowly trotted toward them, but stopped at a safe distance.

"Go away!" shouted Luvvy. "I hate you. That's why I haven't come here before. I wish Papa would sell you."

Sassy whickered softly, as if he could not understand such a rebuff. He came closer, his velvety nose quivering.

Luvvy stared at him resentfully. Not able to understand, Sassy danced lightly on his long legs, like a child showing off. He pushed his nose through the bars hopefully.

Luvvy's feelings softened. She reluctantly petted his muzzle.

"I guess I don't hate you anymore," she admitted. "You didn't know any better because you're only a child yourself."

She felt better now that she had forgiven the colt.

As she scratched his soft nose, a warning drop of water fell on her arm. She looked up quickly. The clouds had dropped lower in greenish-black folds.

"Come, Marylou," she cried. "It's beginning to rain."

By the time they reached the house, a flash of lightning split the sky and let the rain down in a torrent. They rushed for the kitchen door, and a crash of thunder clapped them inside.

The kitchen was empty, so Luvvy knew that Martha was already in the sanctuary of her room and probably under the bed. It was a good thing that Marylou hadn't been left with her.

She took the child to the sitting room and began reading a story to her. But as the storm gathered force, Marylou began to cry.

"There's nothing to be afraid of," Luvvy told her. "I'll cut out some paper dolls for you, and we'll play house with them."

She remembered that Mama would never let them hold scissors during a thunderstorm. She wouldn't even allow them to sew. "Steel draws lightning," she had always warned.

Luvvy said, "No, I can't do that. I know what. Let's go up to the attic and play with my old dolls. I haven't even looked at them all summer."

The rain drummed even louder on the attic roof. As Marylou raised her eyes fearfully to the low ceiling, Luvvy pulled at her.

"Come on. Help me open the trunk."

For a few moments, Marylou forgot the storm as she helped take the little dolls out.

Then there were blue flashes at the windows, followed by a bombardment of thunder. Marylou broke into howls of fright.

Luvvy gave her a little shake. "How can we play with dolls if you're going to act like a baby?" she scolded. "Here! Sit on the bed and change Maid Marian's dress. I'll look through the trunk and find her party gown."

But Marylou clung to her, weeping convulsively.

Luvvy frowned with perplexity. "I'll tell you what, Marylou. If you'll stop crying and not be afraid, I'll give you my dolls—to keep forever and play with whenever you want."

Marylou's shoulders jerked and she stopped in the middle of a deep sob. She rubbed her eyes, then climbed up onto the bed, although she still looked frightened.

As they changed the dolls' dresses, the lightning grew fainter, and the thunder rolled away toward Harpers Ferry.

Luvvy jumped up and dropped Fair Rosamund on the bed.

"The Girls!" she cried. "They must have been out in that. They'll be soaked to the skin."

She lost interest in the dolls. "I hope they were near a farmhouse so they could go inside. But they said they were going back in the mountains."

She beckoned. "Come, Marylou. We better go down and lay out some clothes for them so they can change right away."

"Can I take the dolls?"

"Certainly. I said you could have them, didn't I? I'll carry Fair Rosamund and Lady Jane Grey down. You take Maid Marian—and don't drop her on the stairs."

They went to Regina's room first. Luvvy dug through her bureau drawers while Marylou sat on the floor and played with the dolls. Luvvy selected an embroidered camisole, pantalettes, and a snowdrift of an underskirt. She unfolded a checked-blue gingham dress and draped it over the green bedstead.

"Now we'll go into my room, and I'll get things out for Hetty and Betsey."

By the time they reached the big bedroom across the hall, the sun was shining brightly outside.

Luvvy looked out to see if there was any sign of the hay wagon yet.

"Come quick, Marylou," she called. "There's a beautiful rainbow outside."

Marylou joined her at the window and stared in awe at the colored arch that spanned the valley.

"You see," said Luvvy, "we couldn't have this pretty rainbow if we hadn't had a storm first."

It didn't take her long to find suitable changes for the other two girls because she was familiar with the order in which they arranged their clothing.

"Now we'll go down in the kitchen and heat water. The Girls should soak their feet in hot water so they won't catch cold from being out in the rain."

Martha was back in the kitchen, punching the dying coals with the poker. Her presence didn't daunt Luvvy. She felt new confidence and responsibility.

"That's right, Martha," she said in a commanding voice. "Fire up the stove and put the big kettle on. The Girls will need hot water when they get back because they'll probably be chilled through."

Martha gave her a sharp look, mumbled under her breath, and poked harder. "Yes, Miss Luvvy," she answered obediently. It was the first time she had given that title of respect to Luvvy. And she didn't order her out of the kitchen.

Luvvy's fears about the Girls getting wet were right. They arrived home with sodden clothes and dripping hair.

"I've got everything ready for you," Luvvy greeted them. "I've laid out dry clothes, and I'll bring up a kettle of hot water."

"You angel!" cried Regina.

"I'd hug you if I wasn't so wet," said Betsey.

The Girls scrambled up the stairs like chickens running up the hen-house ladder when they were caught in the rain.

"You ought to be glad you didn't go, Luvvy honey," said Betsey. "We got caught way out in the woods."

"And lightning struck a tree real close to us," added Hetty. "It was terrible. The horses bolted, and Mr. Stonebraker's man had a dreadful time trying to stop them."

"If you zigzag a horse's reins," said Luvvy, "he'll stop soon. But what did you all do?"

"The Stonebraker girls and I dug down into the hay," said Betsy, "but Hetty didn't want to get her dress full of chaff."

"I prayed," said Regina. "I prayed as hard as I could, and the lightning didn't strike us. But we haven't thanked you yet for staying with Marylou. And you were a darling, having everything ready for when we came back."

"We'll do something for you sometime," said Hetty.

"The next time you want something, just ask us," agreed Betsey.

Luvvy saw her chance at last. There was one favor she wanted of the Girls.

"Do you really mean it?" she cried. "You know how much I want to go to the convent this fall. It isn't too

late now. Please, please ask Papa and Mama to let me go."

The Girls hadn't expected this. Maybe a box of candy or a ride on a canalboat.

"But, Luvvy—" Hetty began.

"Let's ask them when they get home," said Betsey. "I'd love to have Luvvy at the convent with me."

"Since I'm the oldest, I'll ask them," said Regina. "After all, they'll have me home now."

But it was a while before Regina could carry out her promise. Mama had so much to tell about the day in Hagerstown.

"There were crowds of people on the streets," she recounted, her black eyes shining. "And I never had such a light blancmange as they served in that restaurant. Wait until you see my new hat." She looked apologetically toward Luvvy. "It's covered with nile-green tulle and has little beads sewed all around the brim."

Luvvy wasn't interested in the hat at the moment. She couldn't wait for Regina to propose the matter. "Can I go to the convent with Hetty and Betsey next month?" she blurted out.

Mama was bewildered. "But you're only twelve—and Miss Luly Violet will have so much sewing to do. Why don't you wait until next year? You'll be even a little older."

Regina joined her. "She has really grown a lot this

153

summer, Mama Della, and the Girls want her. Please let her go."

Papa was not as hard to persuade as Mama. "It will do her good," he said. "Make a lady of her, like it has you all. And Marylou won't be lonely because she'll be kept busy with the baby."

Luvvy smiled knowingly. "And I'm sure it will be a boy."

Papa put his arm around Luvvy's shoulder. "You see, Della, Luvvy really is smart enough to go to boarding school. She knows that the baby is going to be a boy—Clay Savage, Junior."

Mama had to smile. "I guess there's no good reason she shouldn't go to Frederick," she gave in. "I can help Miss Luly with the extra sewing."

XII

One of the Girls

Regina had become absentminded and irritable. She was so different from her natural self. She sometimes snapped at Mama and sat moodily at the table with most of her food untouched.

"There's nothing wrong with me, Mama Della," she retorted. "I'm just thinking about something important."

"It must be important if it's making you so cross," said Papa. "If you have a problem, tell me what it is, and I'll help you solve it."

Regina picked at the pudding in her saucer, rearranging it in little mounds. "Not yet," she answered. "It's something I have to decide for myself."

That very afternoon when she returned from her buggy ride with Alec Garrett, she walked up the brick walk all by herself. Although Alec politely helped her out, he jumped back in the seat and hurriedly drove away.

Regina stopped at the front steps. "I'm not going to marry Alec after all, Mama Della," she announced.

Mama rose from her seat on the porch. "Oh, come now, Regina. Lovers often have quarrels. You'll make up and everything will be fine. Maybe Papa will let you get married earlier."

Regina was firm. "I'm never going to get married. I'm going to become a nun."

Mama was so shocked that she didn't know what to say. Luvvy found words first. "Oh, please don't be a nun, Regina. I want to be a bridesmaid at your wedding. You promised."

"I kept my promise to ask Papa and Mama Della to let you go to Frederick," Regina reminded her, "but I can't keep the other."

"I don't know what your father will say," was all Mama could think to say herself.

Papa had plenty to say. "I'll never agree to such a tomfool thing," he declared, banging the sitting-room table with his fist. He seemed to have forgotten his early objection to the marriage. "Why in the world would a beautiful girl like you want to give up a fine young man who is already a partner in his father's shoe store?"

Regina calmly returned his angry glare. "Because getting married isn't what I really want. I found that out for sure when I took care of Maudie and Mama Della."

"I don't see why you couldn't be happy caring for a husband and family!" roared Papa. "They might get sick sometimes too."

"But I want to nurse all the poor, suffering people I can. I'm going to become a Sister of Charity. I've already written to Emmitsburg."

Papa dropped his hostile manner. He would take Regina on a trip to California. He would buy her one of those new Saxon roadsters. She could marry Alec Garrett tomorrow if she wished, and he would buy a house in Brunswick for them.

"The Sisters of Charity offer me more, Papa," she replied, "a lifetime of happiness, serving others."

Hetty and Betsey were horrified at Regina's decision. They sat in their room and talked in low tones.

"Regina is too beautiful to be a nun," said Betsey. "She could have any man in the valley she wanted."

"But Sister Mary Joseph at Frederick is beautiful," said Luvvy, "and she looks like a saint." She was beginning to approve of the idea of Regina becoming a Sister of Charity. She could see her walking among the wounded soldiers on a battlefield—her cornette fluttering like the wings of an angel.

Hetty slowly shook her head. "I can't see how she can give up Alec Garrett," she sighed.

Luvvy regretted this most of all. She had grown to think of him as a big brother. He had already told her that she could come to Brunswick and ride his roan mare anytime she wished. Now this was all at an end. She probably would never see him anymore except at a polite distance.

But everyone had to agree Regina had made the right decision when she became her old amiable self again.

"It was such a serious decision," she confessed, "and I felt so torn apart. But once I made up my mind for sure, I felt wonderful."

When Miss Luly Violet arrived with her scissors and patterns, the upstairs sitting room was turned into a sewing room. The sewing machine was carried in from the hall, and a litter of threads and fabrics covered the desk and table. For once Hetty didn't complain of the untidiness.

Regina joined in to help Miss Luly and Mama. She had almost finished a blue serge dress for Luvvy's coming school year. As she was adjusting the hem, they heard the sound of horse's hoofs on the road.

Luvvy idly glanced through the window. Then she pulled away from Regina.

"It's Alec Garrett," she cried. "He's stopping here. I'll go see what he wants."

Without another thought for the half-pinned hem, she ran down the steps, across the porch, and down the walk. Perhaps Alec was going to make a last try to change Regina's mind. He had better be warned that it was useless.

Alec smiled pleasantly at Luvvy as he walked to meet her.

"Is Miss Hetty home?" he asked. "It's such a nice day that I thought she might like to take a ride to Harpers Ferry."

"Hetty," repeated Luvvy, wondering if there were something wrong with her ears or Alec's tongue. "Hetty —oh, *Hetty*! I know she will for sure. I'll run ahead and get her. You just wait on the porch."

She raced excitedly up the walk and into the house. She leaped over the piles of fabric and brushed past the table crowded with patterns and pins.

"He's come to take *you* riding, Hetty. *You!*"

For a moment she was afraid that Hetty was going to swallow the pins held between her teeth.

"Oh, I'm so happy," cried Regina. "Alec really deserves someone who can appreciate him."

Hetty blushed deeply as she laid the pins down with a trembling hand.

"B-But are you sure that you don't want him, Regina?"

Regina's only answer was a smile. "Come here, Luvvy, and let me finish the hem," she said.

Hetty ran her fingers through her hair. "But I'll

have to tidy myself first. Oh, oh, I better hurry."

"I'll help you," cried Luvvy, forgetting the hem again.

She followed Hetty to their room and to the mirror over the bureau. Hetty was looking at herself in it critically.

"My hair looks so old-maidish," she complained.

"Please let me comb it," begged Luvvy. "I'll fix it pretty."

She was surprised that Hetty agreed to her help. She ran the comb through the wavy brown hair, then coaxed some of the ringlets loose. "See how pretty they look."

"I do look better with my hair looser," admitted Hetty.

"Pansy says if you lick your finger and rub your eyebrows, it'll make them look darker."

Hetty dipped her finger into the water pitcher and ran it over each brow in turn.

"Now pinch your cheeks to make them red like Mama does. Oh, no, you don't need to. They're so red already."

When Hetty was at last ready to meet Alec, Luvvy had the same feeling as when she finished writing a story she thought particularly good. Then she remembered the hem of her dress.

"And to think that I'll be wearing this dress as a

student at the convent!" she exclaimed proudly as Regina finished the task.

Betsey looked up from lettering name tapes with indelible ink. "You may be disappointed," she remarked. "It isn't all operas and meringues and Commencement Week at Frederick."

"Oh, I know," Luvvy admitted. "Lots of things won't turn out the way I've planned. I'll probably get in trouble often and have to sit on the punishment bench. And I know I'll get homesick at first. Maybe I won't even win a gold medal. But I'll try to make the best of things. I'll just remember how much I wanted to be there with you and Hetty."

Papa and Mama drove the Girls down to the depot the day of their departure for Frederick. It was easier for Luvvy to tell Regina and Marylou and the others good-bye since Mama and Papa would be with her a little longer.

"I haven't time to drive you there in the Machine," Papa had said the day before. "A big order has come in from the west, and I must be at the factory to supervise the packing. You'll have to go by train."

This was a special treat for Luvvy because she hadn't been on a train since Papa had taken her to see the circus in Washington.

As they waited in front of the depot, she felt hot

and cold in turn. She was glad that the new white cotton gloves kept the others from seeing that her hands were moist and trembling. She felt self-conscious in the new blue suit with its raised waistline and longer skirt. It was almost as if she were playing that she was someone else—such as President Taft, skating around the pond.

She looked at Hetty clutching the big box of candy that Alec Garrett had presented to her the night before. Hetty's eyes were sparkling beneath the ringlets over her forehead.

Why, she's herself, thought Luvvy. She's what she's been trying to hide all the time. What fun Betsey and I will have with her at the convent!

"Now, Girls," warned Mama, "don't forget to change trains at Washington Junction."

"We always change there when we go by train," said Hetty.

"And don't speak to strangers," continued Mama.

"Why would we speak to strangers when we don't even know them?" reasoned Betsey.

Papa grinned. "And I'm so worried that Hetty will forget to tell the nuns that she has our permission to correspond with Alec. We don't want her to become a nun too."

There was the wailing of a whistle from beyond the wooded curve. The black train slid around it, slowing for the Weverton stop. As the wheels clanked by, the

162

Savages closed their eyes so they wouldn't get cinders in them.

Luvvy opened hers to see the conductor setting the box below the coach steps.

"All aboard," he called out.

Luvvy tried hard not to weep. She hugged Mama and Papa frantically. She was tempted to cry, "I don't want to go yet. I want to be one of the Children just a little longer."

But she only forced a smile, then followed her older sisters up the steps. Inside the coach, they chose seats on the depot side so they could wave to Mama and Papa. Betsey reversed the red-plush back of a seat with a mighty shove so they could sit facing each other.

Luvvy flattened her nose against the window and waved her initialed handkerchief madly. The engine's bell clanged. A cloud of white steam hid Mama and Papa for a few moments, then lifted.

The train jerked forward. The depot began to move slowly away. Mama and Papa moved with it, still waving. Miss Harriet's house on the hill went past. Everything that had been so familiar to Luvvy moved out of her sight. She was on her way to the convent. She was one of the Girls.

HARPER TROPHY BOOKS
you will enjoy reading

The Little House Books *by Laura Ingalls Wilder*

HARPER & ROW, PUBLISHERS, INC.
49 East 33rd Street, New York, New York 10016